Sepp's Epic Perils & Pitfalls

Sepp Book #1

Sudetenland

To

Kleinerort

*The **Sepp books** are works of fiction.*

The names, characters, businesses, places, events, and incidents are either the product of the author's imagination or used in a fictitious manner. Any resemblance to real living or dead persons is purely coincidental.

I used actual historical events to provide a time frame and appropriate settings for the series of Sepp books.

The character Sepp in the Sepp books is also entirely fictional.

My imagined Sepp does, however, abide by the known facts of the real Sepp's life, and with his permission, I have sometimes quoted from his works and poetry.

helmut s. *Author*

www.Sepp.world

by helmut s.

...delivering a wrinkled, blue red, screaming bundle...

With this O yes does he recall being
pushed into uncertainty his new life.
Nothing but a by-product of making love
where sperm and egg found each other in lust.
And-way-back-then, that was not an easy
time. Later, after he was born, to lead
a normal life, his mother too she lived
togeth'r with a man not too old to learn,

knowing that as it's all going to hell
therefore they might as well visit heaven
before going wherever go they shall.

helmut s

Sepp was born just after World War II, in the Frankenland, in Northern Bavaria. He grew up with Waldemar Schuster, a shoemaker as a father. His mother was Erika Franken, formerly Bauer, a farmer's widow. Both his parents were refugees, deported from their homeland, the Sudetenland. And neither one of his parents had planned to raise another child when he, Sepp happened to arrive nine months after Erika's deportation from the Sudetenland.

What brought Waldemar and Erika together? Asking Erika, as well as Waldemar, both agreed: "It was a surprising, stellar event not explicable by natural or scientific laws and therefore could well be considered a miracle!"

Erika had not expected to meet Waldemar when she accidentally slipped and fell on him at the train station in Ansbach West Germany end of March of 1949. She didn't know the strange man who was catching her. Erika arrived falling into a strange new world with practically nothing aside from the clothing she wore, and the willingness to start over. Erika didn't even have a pair of shoes, but she had Frieda her little girl and all in all a very positive outlook on life, and she had faith. Erika believed that there is a reason for everything in God's world. She needed no additional evidence or proof, aside her being alive after being robbed, beaten, violated and maltreated during the so-called 'open season' not only for Nazis but every German-speaking citizen of the Sudetenland, during the months following the end of WWII.

Whatever crimes happened to Erika, her family and countless victims in the Sudetenland will never be prosecuted by law; some people say it never happened. *"Any act committed between September 1938 and October 28, 1945, the object of which was to aid the struggle for liberty of the Czechs and Slovaks or which represented just reprisals for actions of the occupation forces and their accomplices, is not illegal, even when such acts may otherwise be punishable by law. This law does de facto ensure that no atrocities against Germans during such time period in question will ever be prosecuted in Czechoslovakia."*

In 1949, living in the American Zone of West Germany since 1945, Waldemar realized how well he was off when he counted all those riches money could not buy. Just trying to put a price tag on freedom, he knew he was doing quite well, much better than the many from the East that didn't get to the western zones after WW II. And he was able to work, and his kind of work was everywhere he looked. It was quite obvious that as a shoemaker he was needed any place people had a foot or two. And Erika had feet but no shoes, when she slipped and tumbled from the train on the waiting Waldemar.

What was the Sudetenland like, the 'Heimat' (homeland) Sepp had never seen? German tribes are known to have lived there since the 2nd century AD. For Erika's ancestors, it had been home since the 13th century. The Sudetenland was mainly hilly land, where many German-speaking settlers and their descendants had migrated to farm, cultivate and mine the wild, mountainous edges of the Holy Roman Emperor Charles IV's Kingdom. It had been the home for a large number of German-speaking families for hundreds of years, including the Bauer, the Franken, and the Schuster family.

The Bauer, Franken and Schuster families, together with 100s of German-speaking families trekked to the Sudetenland just about the time that Genghis Khan at the age of 65 fell off his horse and died fighting in China. German speaking families migrated to the Sudetenland while the Europeans were beginning to learn Arabic numbers and Egypt had white slaves who had converted to Islam. The Bauer, Franken and Schuster families built their homes in the Sudeten Mountains at a time when King Edward I of England was forbidding Jews to lend money on interest before he expelled all Jews from his country. The same time-period also became known as the beginning of the 'Little Ice Age,' which lasted 400 years and brought wetter weather and shorter growing seasons to the northern climates. Those were the days when trained tradesman from German-speaking areas followed the call to come to the Sudetenland and settled in the then new territory. The German-speaking settlers and their descendants flourished while dynasties of Bohemian kings came and went, during a period when much of Europe was still uninhabited.

The Sudetenland had been part of the Duchy and Kingdom of Bohemia, and at one era it had belonged to the Austrian-Hungarian Empire. Before 1938 the Sudetenland never belonged to Germany. Over the centuries, the various tribes, including the Slavic tribes, used as their everyday language the Bohemian West Slavic language we know as Czech. They and the German-speaking population lived and worked next to each other. The nation by the name of Tschechoslowakei (Czechoslovakia) was founded in 1918 after the First World War based on the Pittsburg Agreement made by Czech and Slovak expatriates in the United States of America. The Sudetes Mountains and Sudetenland were part of what we know lately as Czech Republic & Slovakia.

Everything changed in the Czechoslovakia when Hitler, with the express written permission of the Italian Prime Minister Benito Mussolini, French Prime Minister Edouard Daladier, and the British Prime Minister Neville Chamberlain invaded the Czech territory and annexed the Sudetenland to the Reich. During the Nazi occupation, anyone German had to provide affidavits of a German family history and that they were not Roma or Jewish. Everyone in the Nazi-occupied Tschechoslowakei was asked to be ready to show the authorities a family tree that went back to their grandparents' era. Every person with a German parentage became a citizen of Hitler's 3rd Reich automatically. All Czech and Slovaks had to carry IDs showing that they were not Jewish or Roma.

What happened to those Roma or Jewish families, as well as anyone who couldn't provide sufficient proof of their heritage? They were subject to arrest, being forced to work in factories, in mines, or sent to Concentration Camps. It is a rough guess that from about 300,000 Jews only about 30,000 survived the Nazi occupation of the Sudetenland. No one knows the real numbers. The same goes for the Roma families; we don't know how many perished between the years 1938 and 1945. Supposedly there were tens of thousands of Romani families living in the country. Both the Jews and the Roma were part of the population living right next door and mixed in with Sudeten-Germans and Czech people, made up of West

Slavic ethnic groups and native speakers of the Czech language. What happened to those unable to verify being German during the Nazi days? Nobody knows the actual number of people's lives brought to an end during 1938 through 1945 in the Tschechoslowakei. It is therefore entirely understandable that during the years of Nazi occupation 1938 through 1945, many people not only Czechs had stored up anger, and developed a deep-seated severe dislike, for every man, woman, and child with a German name. It did not matter if those had been Sudeten-Germans living in the hills since the Middle Ages.

What about the Czech government officials in exile? Already in 1942, Czechoslovak president-in-exile Beneš wrote: *"The words Sudeten, Sudetenland, and Sudete will forever in our Czech lands be connected with Nazi brutality toward we Czechs and toward democratic Germans before and after the fateful crisis of 1938."*

How did the defeat of Nazi Germany in the spring of 1945 change the life in Sudetenland? That's when radical groups of Czechs and sympathizers saw their time for revenge had come. It was payback time for the Nazi takeover in 1938. In the end, the Sudetenland ceased to exist. All German names got replaced, in an attempt to stamp out forever the memory of German control, never mind that for hundreds of years those Sudeten-Germans and their families had been at home in (Bohemia, Moravia, and Silesia) their Sudetenland.

Groups of Czech militias in retaliation inflicted horrible acts against many of the Sudeten-German people within their reach. Forgotten was that for more than 600 years German-speaking families had lived in the Sudetenland and had been good neighbors. Now Sudeten-German families were driven from their ancient homes, many being killed, beaten and often violated by groups of revenge-seekers with rather questionable intentions. Under the pretense of vengeance for war crimes, and looking for Nazis, those mobs often didn't know the people they hurt. They, however, recognized their enemy as anyone with a German name or German-speaking. Murder, violence and the molestation of females became the order of the day.

If that sounds familiar, it matches the routine of warfare since before biblical times: 'The winner takes all!' And losers have little say in whatever the winner does with them because he can do so.

What was Waldemar's life like before he landed in West Germany's American sector? Waldemar Schuster had been making shoes for those who could afford new shoes in both World War I and II, and he expertly repaired shoes as needed. Waldemar was a tall, well-built man. He was a typical city person, living and working in town with a strong desire to travel and visit other cities. Waldemar visited members of his family who lived in the big city, in Prague, on a regular basis. He had traveled a lot within the European countries, as well as one trip to South America, to Argentine, visiting relatives. At the end of the Second World War, he was in his mid-50s, although he looked much younger. He had a square face, a few earned wrinkles, blue eyes, and straight short gray-blond hair.

Waldemar was from a long line of shoemakers. He was a shoemaker, as his father and his grandfather had been. Waldemar had inherited the Schuster Shoemaker Shop located in the Schuster building from his father. His family had owned the Schuster Building located in downtown Troppau for many generations. Waldemar enjoyed living in Troppau. He grew up in Troppau, a city created in 1224 that was once the capital of Silesia. Ever since his ancestors migrated to the area, the Schuster family had been making shoes and boots for Royals, noblemen, soldiers, farmers, and anyone else. It was Waldemar's grandfather who had talked about having filled an order of 'leather corsets' for the people up at the castle at one time. Surely, over the years, there had been some other unusual requests too, but making and repairing shoes was what the Schuster family did best.

Shoemakers with the Schuster name had been cladding the feet of people in and around Troppau with proper footwear long before Juan de Oñate's days. The explorer who in the name of the Spanish crown and with permission from the church, chopped the natives' feet off in the then New World, now known as North America, and sold the women and children from Acoma Sky City into slavery.

In April of 1945, Waldemar Schuster employed a handful of trained shoemakers, two journeyman, and four apprentices. Word was out that the Eastern Front was crumbling and the Wehrmacht retreating.

It was on a crisp sunny spring morning, Rudolf Schuster, Waldemar's father, came looking for his son with a significant premonition: "All last night and until daybreak, our Nazi leadership has been leaving town! I watched from my bedroom window the vehicles and the men with stern faces. Everyone is heading home towards their Fatherland." "You did?" Waldemar asked. Rudolf was looking straight into his son's eyes, and in a serious tone, he told him: "You must get Karl and Traude! Better yet, get Karl out of the country, take the gold with you, he will need it. He must leave Europe, tell him to go to South West Afrika or even better South Amerika." On that very same morning, Waldemar Schuster handed his shop back over to Rudolf, his 80year old father, who, together with two of his employees, was now in charge. Each of these men had been working at the Schuster Shoemaker Shop for more than 25 years, and the eldest, Manfred was married to Renate, Waldemar's sister. Renate and her husband lived with Rudolf upstairs in the Schuster Building.

Waldemar topped off the gas tank of his motorcycle and loaded the sidecar with smoked meat, Schinken, Speck and sausages, a few loaves of bread, canned beans, canned pears, and two bags of flour, cigarette paper and tobacco. Then Waldemar raided the savings box, the one buried under a rock in the backyard. He did follow his father's instructions and took the small bag full with gold Kronen and Ducats, mainly Hungarian and Austrian coins. And he got on the road towards Berlin. Waldemar was telling himself over and over "I must get to the German capital before the Russians do!" Waldemar's mission was to get to his kids, to Traude and Karl, and to get them both out of Berlin. Just in case, he took along papers containing orders to make a certain number of Officer's boot for the Schutzstaffel also known as SS. The signatures on those orders were impressive, the content of no value other than to allow him if stopped to prove who he was and why he was heading to Berlin. Karl had gotten him the papers, to make sure his father would be allowed to travel anytime to Berlin, without too many questions asked whenever stopped at any checkpoint.

Waldemar left Troppau in the nick of time because two days later the first Russian soldiers reached Troppau, also known as Opava. On his motorcycle, a 1943-BMW-R-75 with sidecar, in typical April weather of mixed sunshine and rain; it took Waldemar two full days to get from Troppau to Berlin. When he got there, it was a shocking experience. He remembered Berlin from many previous visits, last time a year ago, to be still an impressive city. The Berlin he entered now was a very depressive, bombed out town, with ruins where once magnificent buildings lined the roads.

As he passed the street where Traude's apartment used to be, the place Waldemar's wife, Emma, had stayed until the bombing raid, three months earlier, he stopped. What he saw was nothing but rubble, between two walls. The four story apartment building had received a direct hit while his daughter was at work, only her mother, Waldemar's wife, Emma, was home. Neighbors, mainly women, as men were in very short supply in the city, had heard Emma's screams. Following her voice, they had dug Waldemar's wife out from under the bricks and dirt. Traude's mother had died shortly after, in her daughter's arms, at the Charité Hospital succumbing to her injuries. "But why did Emma have to go to Berlin, in the first place? She would have been perfectly safe, at home in the Sudetenland!" Waldemar was asking himself, drying his face, as tears rolled from his eyes. Waldemar remembered his wife insisting on being closer to their daughter, to Traude, who planned to get married that year. Emma wanted to be close to their son Karl too.

"Gott steh Dir bei!" (May God be with you!) He prayed, while finding his way along the roads, a slalom course, carefully avoiding those bomb craters. He drove around piles of rubble scattered all over those streets, once the avenues for parades and the pride of the Reich. Much of Berlin was a grim field of destruction. The Allied Forces' carpet-bombing had spared only a few buildings. Waldemar pressed on. He saw the swarm of bombers in the sky, explosions like thunder, all in the distance, not too far, but far enough. Waldemar didn't care about what might happen to him. He was in Berlin to rescue both his two kids and get them out of the German Capital.

Waldemar went first to Traude's workplace the Charité, a world famous hospital. There he found his daughter.

Edeltraud Schuster, nicknamed Traude, was by then 30 years young, and Karl, 35 years old. Traude looked tired, but she was prepared to do her duties like all the hospital staff, doctors and nurses alike did. Traude was tall, like her brother Karl, like her father. She was slim, with an oval face, blue eyes, and blond hair. She was known to be hardworking, practical, gentle, generous and intelligent. Waldemar wished now and there that his daughter wouldn't be so stubborn. At the time she was engaged to a doctor at the hospital, and the two had plans to get married soon. Because she was a nurse at the Charité, Traude was not going to leave her post: "...I am a nurse! My place is with my patients!" was her response to Waldemar's plea: "Please come with us, Karl and me, let's get out of Berlin, as long as we can get out of here! You do remember what happened to Mama?" Waldemar tried and tried. All of his appeals to her common sense and sense of self-preservation fell on closed ears. Traude was not going to change her mind. "I'm staying with my patients! ...so what? I am at a hospital! ... and a Russian invasion doesn't make any difference!" had been her answer and "I am going to stay with my man, my husband-to-be!" Waldemar didn't like her answers but had to respect her wish. Traude insisted that hospitals were safety zones according to the Geneva Convention, so unless being hit by a stray bomb, as it had happened to her apartment building, she felt she was safe. Waldemar knew how unyielding his daughter could be. He was aware that food was in very short supply, in the city. Therefore he gave his daughter almost all of the provisions he had brought along in the sidecar. Traude was delighted to see the loaves of bread, the sides of Speck and meat, the smoked sausages, the flower and the canned goods. Traude agreed with her father that Karl would be much safer any place but at the Reichstag, guarding Adolf Hitler.

Listening to bombs falling in the not too far distance, Waldemar drove over to Karl's quarters. Fortunately, Karl Schuster was off duty that day. Karl looked just like Emma, his mother, tall, blond hair and blue-eyed, never mind that his sister Traude insisted that he looked more like Waldemar, his father. Karl had been an Honor Guard at the Reichstag since early 1940. He believed his father when Waldemar said: "If you stay here, you will not live one day past the Russian arrival! As soon as the Russians see your uniform near Hitler's hideout, you are dead!" Karl had never been in combat, but as being a soldier and part of Hitler's Leibstandarte, an SS member, staying and defending Berlin he knew was a suicide mission. Not only did Karl respect Waldemar's words but he was most grateful for having an opportunity to leave Berlin. Karl was fully aware of the fact that leaving equaled desertion, the abandonment of duty without permission and if caught it meant certain death. But leaving with his father at least there was a slim chance that he may live to see his very own children growing up, of which he had none so far. Staying in Berlin was unquestionable certain death. With that in mind, it didn't take much effort to convince Karl to leave Berlin the same day. Both Waldemar and Karl knew the outcome of the war. Karl trusted his father's vision implicitly.

The two left the city on Waldemar's motorcycle within the hour. They didn't know it, but it was in the nick of time on April 13th. Two days later, the Soviet Army was getting ready to level Berlin. They started with what some called 'a most spectacular display of artillery.' Others called it a 'bloody affair.' Waldemar was praying for Traude, and that she was right that the Charité hospital will be treated according to the Geneva Conventions. But now first, he had to save his son Karl and to get him to and on Swiss soil.

Leaving Berlin, it was snowing, later changing to rain, April weather. And it took them all day, 16 hours of driving, to get to the Swiss border. South of the Bodensee, the sun was shining, here and there a few white clouds in the blue sky. At the border crossing into Switzerland, Waldemar said to Karl: "Auf Wiedersehen! Sohn machs gut!" (Good Bye! Son take care!) There was no big goodbye. Waldemar gave his son the bag of gold coins.

And after handing Karl his beloved motorcycle, he knew that he had done all he could, to save his son's life. From here on, Karl's future was up to the powers above. Waldemar's vision for Karl was to get to Marseille and aboard a freighter to South America.

What saved Waldemar's son's life was that Karl Schuster did just as his father had suggested. He was slowed down. The traffic on many roads was going the other way. It was as everyone was heading towards Germany. Karl nearly missed the boat! As he worried about getting to his ship, Karl toyed with the idea of joining the French Foreign Legion, changing his name and identity, until whenever. Karl finally arrived in Marseille and got aboard a ship to South America. He did make his way to Brazil and from there on to Argentine. Karl Schuster made out okay, staying with German families, and making the best of it. Letters he sent to the Red Cross trying to locate his father's address took many months by boat to arrive in Germany. Return mail took equally long.

“Yes, ‘argh!’ Internet and e-mail didn’t exist back then!”

Communications between the continents were very slow. Karl Schuster returned to West Germany in the early 1950s, after the Nuremberg War Trials, and after the winning parties initial thirst for revenge and the call for ‘let’s kill all SS members alike’ had been stilled. In 1952, a large electronics company in Munich hired Karl. And that’s where Karl Schuster worked until his retirement.

After handing Karl his motorcycle, Waldemar stayed on in Bavaria. He had planned to return home, to the Sudetenland, to his shop, his family, and his workers. Waldemar Schuster was on the train home to Troppau. At the Bahnhof in Ulm, a group of men in uniform got on the train. He listened to their conversation, and it was all about the Eastern Front and that there were reports that the Russians were winning. Waldemar remembered the bombing of Prague, in February. The more he heard, the more he knew that going east was no longer an option. Troppau was not where he wanted to be at the time.

Waldemar Schuster's urge for staying alive, and not being stupid enough to attempt to get back to Troppau in 1945, made the decision easy. He got off the train in Ansbach. Waldemar never got on the next train home to Troppau. No! Waldemar had no plans to rush back to the Sudetenland and into the arms of the Russian forces because it wouldn't have helped the situation. Waldemar by now like so many others was sick and tired of the war. He was prepared to wait for the end of the fighting right there in Ansbach. Another option was to travel to the nearby city of Nuremberg. He didn't want to be in any bigger city because all cities had lately been subject to daily carpet bombing. He wondered: "Maybe I should have gone with Karl." He hoped for the best for everyone at home. Waldemar knew with his dad Rudolf in charge of the shop all was in good hands. Waldemar was however worried about his two younger brothers. Both were in the German merchant marine, and he had not heard from them now in nearly a year.

The day after arriving in Ansbach, on a fine but frigid April day, knowing that the money in his pockets shall run out fast, Waldemar looked for work. He got hired on the spot at the first shoemaker shop he visited and applied for work, because of his much-needed skills. The pay was excellent, but as money lost its value with every minute, the Reichsmark was useless. The shop owner provided Waldemar with a place to sleep, and best of all, the owner's family was delivering farm products daily to support those four shoemakers, including Waldemar, at the shop.

The end to the insane war was a matter of days now. On May 2nd, 1945 the news that the Russians had taken control of Berlin spread fast.

It was a pleasant surprise when the American military vehicles rolled in and through Ansbach, after having set up headquarters at the airfield outside of Ansbach a week earlier. After a short fight, Ansbach's Hitler Youth finally surrendered. People were relieved including Waldemar Schuster.

When the first group of American soldiers came into the store, Waldemar was sitting with his back to the door. He was replacing a shoe-sole. On the command "Hands Up, Hände hoch!" everyone in the store raised their hands to the ceiling, and as Waldemar saw the other cobblers raising their hands high up in the air, he did the same. Then two young Americans inspected the shoemaker shop. After looking around, they watched Waldemar using wooden nails to attach the sole to a pair of shoes. Even in his much worn Wehrmacht's uniform pants, he was nothing less or more but a perfectionist when it came to shoes.

The Same day, a few hours later, the two soldiers came back and brought several pairs of boots which needed work. Those two soldiers waited for the repairs to be done, one of them spoke some German. The workmen in the shop attended to those other pairs of boots, while Waldemar fixed one pair. Here the soles needed to be reattached at the toe-end to the upper-leather. It wasn't the last time he got to do some work for the newly arrived soldiers, who overpaid him with American cigarettes.

What was life in West Germany like after 1945? At the end of the war, Germany was divided into four sectors: The British Zone, the American Zone, the French Zone and the Soviet Zone. All of Bavaria was in the American Zone. Waldemar heard stories about the people in Schwabenland, and how the French North African troops mistreated the female German population in Stuttgart. Waldemar, however, was never treated badly, by any of the American soldiers.

Waldemar Schuster as part of the group of 'Refugees from the Sudetenland' was asked to move into a Lager, the camp for people deported from the East. The Lager was also in Ansbach, Bavaria. All Sudeten-Germans, as they arrived in Ansbach, talked about the situation back home in Troppau and Prague, and the news was no good news. Waldemar realized how fortunate he was by getting off the train in time.

Having no home to return to, Waldemar kept on doing, what he was doing since being a boy, a young man, doing what his family had been doing since the dark ages. Waldemar created shoes, perfectly fitting shoes according to the pair of feet they had to protect. Often enough as new leather was scarce, he made out of several old pairs, a new pair. People needed shoes, even if they could get away with wearing little on their feet in the summer, winter was guaranteed to come, and without shoes, no one could get far.

Then one day in 1947, he repaired the shoes for an older frail looking refugee woman, who had just arrived from Troppau, and she told him: "Many Germans, from the old families, are incarcerated at the 'Collection Camp,' the place that used to be the Nazi Slave-Labor Camp. At the Troppau Camp, good people are being abused, tortured, and raped." She said: "Listen, Herr Schuster, it's only the lucky ones who get hanged, or killed by other means, that lets them escape from the misery!" Hearing that, he gratefully thanked God that he got to the American Zone in 1945 and that he never had to experience the Troppau camp, notorious for the maltreatment of Sudeten Germans after the end of WWII. And Waldemar was concerned about his father, as well as troubled by the uncertainty as to Manfred and Renate's whereabouts. It was quite unlikely that anyone of his family or from his shop was still in the Schuster Building. Waldemar was perturbed thinking of all those people he knew since early childhood because he grew up in Troppau. Waldemar Schuster went to school in Troppau. He did business in Troppau. And deeply moved and emotionally hurt he was asking himself: "What did we do to make them Czechs hate us so much?"

What was it like to be German-speaking and to live in Sudetenland after April 1945? As the German front disintegrated, wave after wave of soldiers and groups of more or less armed militias had followed the retreating Wehrmacht. The groups of Russian soldiers were all too busy rushing towards Berlin to capture Hitler. They did not spend much if any time, as they passed through the Sudetenland, now Czech territory. The Russian troops looked forward to getting some rest. Some did their duty as told and raped the one or the other German-speaking woman. Easy prey easy found, helpless unprotected by any man. The law was on the soldiers' side. It was very much expected that they would hurt those mothers of present day and future German soldiers where it counts, namely by degrading their self-respect. Violating and humiliating their prey by using and abusing their bodies was just another means of getting even with the German Volk. After 1945, German-speaking women had no rights in the new Czech Republic. Some women defended themselves and were killed. Others killed themselves, and the rest endured whatever happened with and to them.

There were no cameras or video recorders capturing the suffering Erika and Heidi endured, on the Bauer farm. "And if so? Would it have mattered, would it have changed the outcome?" So much that followed the end of World War II, in the Sudetenland, has conveniently left out of today's history books. It wasn't relevant to the rest of the world. Almost all military-age men were either dead or in POW camps, and the number of German males in the population was pretty much limited to young boys and old men. Therefore the brunt of all attacks and abuse were against the women.

But, what about the men and boys in Sudetenland? Sepp read about the massacre at Postelberg, now called Postoloprty, based on reports by eyewitnesses, where in June 1945 a few thousand Germans were slaughtered, thus did include some boys. "The commander of the Czech troops, ordered the boys to be shot as well." The oldest was 15, the youngest 12. They were killed -- in full view of the others, who were held back at gunpoint. The Czechs didn't use machine guns, but their rifles, so it took a long time to kill those kids. There was no instant access to information; there were no newspapers or radio reporters who made the suffering in Sudetenland public. There was no Internet, no smartphones, no instant video calls. It took many years for people who experienced the Postoloprty massacre on June 6, 1945, to come forward and to tell their story. Because of people were ashamed to admit what had happened to them, many didn’t disclose for years the sacrifices they had made and the pain they had endured. And others just couldn't admit having taken part in the forceful expulsion of Germans from the Sudetenland. What happened to a few million Sudeten-Germans didn't matter in the bigger picture of war and peace. After all, Nazi Germans had been the scourge of evil. Why should any of the Sudeten-Germans have deserved international sympathy?

Where was Erika in 1945? The only home, Erika knew was the Bauer's Bauernhof, the place Sepp's ancestors had called home, for many centuries. The Bauer family had owned the 30-acre parcel in the mountainous area of the Sudetenland, also known as Sudeten Mountains, since the year 1271 AD.

In the early spring of 1945, except the livestock, cows, horses, pigs, goats, chickens, rabbits and two dogs, only Erika and her sister Heidi were on the farm, the Bauer farm, and residence.

All buildings at the Bauer Bauernhof had extremely steep roofs, to allow the snow to slide off. The main house dated to the 15th century, from stones quarried on the same property. A big wooden barn was on the other side the yard, behind the manure heap. The barn was much newer; last rebuilt when Erika was a child. It was used to store the hay, grains, seeds, firewood, troughs, barrels, baskets, and all the farming tools and equipment as well as some items too good to throw out from bygone days, collected by parents and grandparents. And off to the side in the corner, covered up with a tarp were those two motorcycles, belonging to the two Bauer boys, Erika's brothers, next to the ladder wagon and the carriage.

The Bauernhof sat like an open U-shape on a knoll overlooking a spring fed creek and the land below. The stables, cow barn, and pig sty were old, consisting of three buildings next to each other. There was plenty of space for the pigs, a lot of room for the cows, and a separate area with stalls for 12 horses. The walls were solid stone. The floors were also made of stone, and sloped to allow for the liquid manure to run off and out under the doorways straight into the manure heap out front. In the past, the Bauer family raised cows and produced milk and cheese products for sale in the village. By the time Erika was born, there were never more than four cows. The stables for the horses had a dozen stalls, thus too was because, in the last century, the Bauers' were into breeding and selling Kladrubers. Next, to the big barn, there was the new lean-to-shelter. Lorenz with the help of his sons Hans and Fritz had finished it in the spring of 1939 during the Nazi invasion into the Sudetenland. The wooden structure provided cover from the elements for all animals in the paddocks. Next to the lean-to was the chicken coop.

In the valley facing the south side of the farm, at the foot of the knoll, a fast-flowing brook divided the flat acreage into two sections. The right side was grassland. On the left side were three small, tilled and planted fields. In 1945, the Bauers grew potatoes, wheat, and cabbage. The farmland was bordered at the north and the west by massive mountains tops. To the east side, a good size hill separated two canyons. The ridgeline was the border between the Bauer and the Bartsch property. No steps or pathways lead to the other side, only the trails created by wildlife such as wild boar, foxes, rabbits, and deer. A mixture of deciduous and coniferous evergreen trees covered much of the hilly areas on all sides. On the incline towards the neighbor, wild blueberry bushes were in bloom. That was also where Erika harvested the best edible mushrooms every fall. The nearest neighbor, Ralf Bartsch, was more than 3 kilometers away following the roads on both sides of the hill separating their properties. It was a long walk down to the valley past the large, old, leaning oak tree and back up the neighbor's road through the gorge along the river. Past the blueberry bushes, following the deer path up the steep hillside and over the wooded ridge, the neighbor's farm was less than half the distance, 500 meters up the hill and 500 meters down on the other side.

Behind the main house, a few dozen fruit trees had been planted over the years. Earlier in the day, Erika had watched some wild bees visiting the blossoming cherry trees. Plum, apple and pear trees were soon getting ready to bloom too. Between the orchard of planted fruit trees and the house, Erika's had her garden. Here she grew carrots, onions, garlic, beets, and herbs. It was all fenced in, to keep animals out.

The Bauer's Bauernhof was tucked away at the end of a canyon in the Sudeten Mountains. The nearest town was Burgstadt, a small town below an old castle, a 25 kilometer trip, depending on road conditions which frequently changed in the mountains. From the farm, it was only 4km to the next village, a cluster of 12 homes, the schoolhouse, and the church. To get to the big city Prague, that was a day trip. A long journey, Erika had never been to Prague.

Erika's parents Lorenz Bauer and Marta Bauer were visiting family members in Prague. Lorenz and Marta were due back any day now. Lorenz and Marta Bauer had five grown up kids, two sons, and three daughters. Heidi was the oldest, and she was tall, with medium blond wavy hair, and men found her to be very attractive. Then there was the simple, modest looking Erika, and Olga the smartest of the kids and also the youngest. The two sons were Hans and Fritz, both younger than Erika but older than Olga.

Erika Franken, the second oldest daughter in the Bauer family, was only 154 cm tall (5'1") and weighed about 65 kg, Erika was short, plump but not fat. She was in her early forties. Her round weather-tanned face, friendly smile and large brown eyes were merely a reflection of her entire body structure, and every part from her strong arms to her rounded body expressed good health and happiness. As far as she remembered, Erika had never cut her thick dark blond hair. Not braided it was going past her knees. She was hard working and cheerful. Erika always had a positive outlook of life on the farm. Heavy work had hardened her hands, but not her heart. Erika was most gentle, soft and caring whenever needed to be. Erika believed that all people were good. And she meant it when she said to her sister Heidi: “There is a reason and there is a purpose for everything! God and Mother Nature are still in control of all life, the beginnings, and endings, all we can do is work and pray!” Her sister Heidi agreed “Oh ja sister! You are right! You know!”

From the Bauer kids, Erika was the only one married. She had married her childhood friend Helmut on the day before he went to war. “To have someone to come back to!” he had said. And once Helmut returned, Erika was going to move in with him, on his farm, the one he had inherited as being the only son of the Franken family. And they had talked about having kids, and about raising horses because he loved his horses. They had also talked about having a herd of goats. Erika loved goats, goat milk, goat cheese, goat meat, anything goat. And Helmut had agreed because the Franken farm had much land and most of it was hilly. It was ideal for goats but not for growing crops.

About the Franken family and the farm, Helmut's place, the farm Erika planned to move to, once her husband returned from the Wehrmacht. The Franken family came as their name said from Frankenland a long time ago. They owned and operated the first sawmill in the area, located the middle of old growth of trees. A waterwheel powered the mill. The Franken family had been supplying the wood for most homes built in the nearby village, including the schoolhouse and the church, as well as the wood for many of the surrounding farms.

The mountain range to the north of the Franken property had been mined for gold since the Celtic times or even earlier. In 1939 the Nazis had confiscated that part of the Franken farm. Ever since the Nazis had been tunneling into the mountain, the rumor was they were creating an underground factory. The area had been 'off limits,' forbidden territory ever since the Nazis took over. Erika wasn't sure what was going on there. She hadn't been in that part of Helmut's property since her school days. Back then Helmut had taken her on horseback to the old mine shafts. There wasn't much to see, just holes in the solid rock formation, and dirt piles and rock out front. She always liked Helmut. He was the only one in school who didn't call her names, including 'Dummkopf' her nickname back then and there. Helmut too was a slow learner in school, but he was smart when it came to animals and anything farming. Erika was thinking of talking with Helmut's parents. They lived on the other side of the village about 6km up in the mountains.

Somehow it might have been a good thing that she didn't have the ability to contact his parents, by phone or other means. Helmut's mother was from Romania, his father, a German-Jew. Nice people, good people, yet the tide of change didn't care for 'good or nice' anymore. Helmut's parents had been able to fool the Nazi authorities with some papers Helmut's dad had printed up, using names from the graveyard. But now because he was German and she was married to him, they too vanished in the tidal wave of hatred against Sudeten-Germans in 1945.

Erika's husband, was in the Wehrmacht, just like her two brothers Hans and Fritz. With Hitler's annexation of the Sudetenland and providing all Sudeten Germans with the Third Reich citizenship, automatically all healthy and able-bodied men were drafted into military duties for the Reich. In 1935 Hitler had introduced military conscription, by 1938 he had 36 infantry divisions of 600,000 men, after adding the Sudetenland in 1939 the German Army had 98 divisions. Yes, and aside from all 20-year-old plus, who had to do their military duty, a good number of non-German men, therefore exempted from service, did volunteer to fight on the German side as well.

As the war was going on, Erika hadn't heard much from any of her men. It was over six months that they had gotten a letter from Hans, who said that they Fritz and he, were okay. However, none of them had heard about or seen Helmut since 1943. Erika and Heidi were still waiting for Olga, their younger sister. Olga was supposed to be back from her visit to the nearby town. While waiting for the rest of the Bauer family to come home, it was up to Heidi and Erika to take good care of the Bauer Bauernhof.

Erika was thinking about changing her *EBr* monograms on all her clothing to *EBF* to reflect her new name, the Franken name, Helmut's name!

It rained overnight, and the air was fresh and clean that morning. With clear skies overhead, Erika Franken mentioned to her sister Heidi Bauer: "It truly looks like a lovely day. I can smell it. Change is in the air."

How true, the world turned upside down for Erika and Heidi, on that April day in 1945, when Ralf Bartsch, their neighbor visited. But it wasn't the change Erika had in mind. As they had no telephone on the farm, not even a radio, they were always eager to get some news, to hear about the outside world. Both dogs, shepherds were meeting in the middle of the farm's entrance gate, at the end of their chain looking towards the valley. They were listening. Heidi Bauer heard the horse's trap-trap too. It was a man in a one-horse buggy. She called Erika, who told each dog to get in his doghouse and stay. Both dogs, well trained listened and followed Erika's orders.

The women were waiting to see the visitor round the bend of the dirt road leading up and on to them. As he came closer, they recognized him. It was their neighbor. Heidi and Erika welcomed the visitor as he came to a halt in front of them. His horse was sweaty, slobbering from the mouth from racing up the hill. Heidi offered to get some hay and a bucket of water. When Ralf Bartsch, their neighbor asked about Lorenz and Marta and found out that they hadn't returned from Prague, he was very concerned, because as he said: "Prague is no longer a safe place to be, for anyone German."

Ralf Bartsch, their neighbor, spoke fluent German. He was from Siebenbürgen, Transylvania in Romania with a Czech wife and two girls age 12 and 14. Answering Erika's question as to the whereabouts of his kids, he told them: "I'm on my way back home. I dropped the kids off at their grandparents, you know, at my wife's parents!" Erika and Heidi Bauer, both knew his wife's family, the Primátors as a very well-of-to-do Czech family in Burgstadt. And Herr Bartsch explained further: "It's just a hundred meters to the schoolhouse from the Grandparents' home. Understandable my wife insists that they go to school there!"

He was changing the subject to the reason why he had stopped in. Herr Bartsch came to warn Erika and Heidi: "Do not do any travel to town, not even to the village in the valley below!" As Erika listened to him, she was panic-stricken. He told them about rather unspeakable acts, true horror stories happening since the German troops had been defeated. Ralf Bartsch wanted to make sure that they, his neighbors, were aware of those most recent changes, and told them about daily attacks against Sudeten Germans and all German-speaking inhabitants of the Sudetenland. When Herr Bartsch asked them: "How is Olga doing, we enjoyed having her tutoring our daughters, she is an excellent teacher." Erika had a sad look on her face while Heidi answered: "Olga went for a ride to Burgstadt but hasn't come back!" And Erika added: "Neither has Schwarzer, her horse! We are worried. We pray that nothing happened to them. Schwarzer always knows his way home. You know!" Herr Bartsch didn't say what was going through his mind. Outside of Burgstadt, he had passed by a camp with maybe 20 men. He did see them cutting up a horse for meat. The legs were dark. The carcass was skinned. May that have been Olga's Schwarzer? No! Ralf shook his head. He was not going to tell Heidi or Erika what he saw, and what he was afraid of may have happened. And if that was Olga's horse, what may have happened to Olga? Herr Bartsch with a "Listen, please do not leave the security of your farm, do not go searching for Olga, she will be back when things are better! If Russian soldiers come up here, let them search the property, don't fight them, and you should be okay." With that Herr Bartsch turned his buggy around and headed back down the dirt road.

In late April of 1945, a group of twelve relatively organized Russian soldiers raided the Bauer farm. They shot and killed both of Erika's dogs because they were barking and protecting the property. Erika and Heidi were alone on their family's farm. Both wore their traditional clothing of skirt, blouse, vest, and apron.

Unprepared for what might come next. A stunned Erika and a frightened Heidi experienced their moment of getting ready to visit their final resting place, as those Russian soldiers took over the Bauer farm. Two hostile-looking soldiers had their rifles pointed at the two petrified women, who utterly frightened raised their hands straight up in the air, as they stood side by side in front of the manure heap. But they didn't get shot like the dogs earlier. It wasn't so much the view of the rifles, but the deadly looking shiny bayonets, reflecting the sun rays, mounted beneath the muzzles, which horrified Erika the most. When Heidi in Russian asked: "What have we done to you? Why the guns?" She was instructed by one of the men "Shut up, or...!" The other soldiers spread out, systematically searched in the barn, the haystacks, the stable and the house, including the cellar and upstairs, without finding any German soldiers, because there weren't any to be found. When one of the soldiers came back and asked Erika: "Frau, where men, your men?" Heidi answered and explained in Russian, "There are no men on the farm but only us, me Heidi and my sister Erika!" He looked at her and nodded his head.

Finished with the exhaustive search, satisfied that there were no men, no guns, only two scared women on the farm, those Russians acted a lot less threatening. They directed both shaken women into the house, the kitchen and demanded food and drink. Two soldiers went out and came back with six headless chickens. Erika plucked them and cleaned those hens in front of a handful of the men, who watched her every move. Heidi prepped vegetables. Once Heidi was done with putting pots with potatoes and cabbage on the fire, one of the soldiers, apparently, the one in charge took her aside. He had noticed that Heidi understood Russian quite well. He ordered her: “Frau, get me some wine from the cellar.” True they had two barrels of apple wine. Heidi responded “I do so, I get it for you from the cellar!” in fluent Russian. He looked at her. He listened. He nodded his head and told her: “Frau! Go! Davai!” and then after lighting a candle so he could see, he followed Heidi down the steps into the dark. As time crept forward, Erika got the impression that the soldiers hanging out in the kitchen were making bets on how long it may take their leader to return. It wasn’t too long before Heidi returned. She didn't bring any wine. She was short of breath. Her face was red. Her hair was undone and her clothing in disarray.

The man who had escorted her down followed her, his uniform jacket over his arm, buttoning his pants. As he did so, he said something to his men in Russian. At first, Erika didn't understand, what he said. As she looked at the soldiers' faces, whatever he said was putting a grin on some faces and a large smirky smile on others. Listening better, now she understood. He was praising Heidi, saying: "The Frau good, take Frau, go, I call when food cooked!" Erika also understood that he talked about "Davai! Fick Frau! Davai!" He ordered his men to take Heidi over into the barn until dinner was ready. He was going to watch Erika who was terror-stricken, worried about her sister Heidi, and not sure what she was going to do if any of those men dared to lay their hands on her.

The men then left with her sister, who had understood every word. She knew what they were up to. It was Heidi who was giggling and talking with the young men in Russian. She was asking each one about their families and their hometowns in Russia, and how long they had been in the horrible war. Heidi did not sound the least bit scared, and if she was, she surely didn't show it. Erika admired her older sister. Heidi always had been different, she could handle men anytime, and she could surely handle these. Heidi had always referred to men as nothing more or less than big boys who need to be mothered. Four soldiers who had made sure no enemy would enter the perimeters, those who had been doing guard duty for the past 2 hours, came to the kitchen. They smelled food, but their leader instructed them: "Go to the barn first, get some, see tall Frau, and have four others who are ready, have gotten some already, to go on duty!"

Heidi was back just over an hour later. She acted like nothing had happened and helped Erika feeding their self-invited guests. Both women made sure the dozen hungry young men got dinner. While the men were eating, Heidi suggested that the men have a bath. Erika got busy pumping water into buckets, while Heidi, carried them in and filled up four large pots. They heated the water on the kitchen stove, enough water to fill two bathtubs. When Heidi announced that they only had one piece of soap and everyone would have to share, she had some of the boys laughing. Then Heidi went and brought out clean underwear and socks that belonged to her father and her brothers. She piled the fresh clothes up on the kitchen table.

"What am I going to do with these men?" Erika asked herself and finally asked her sister. And Heidi told Erika: "Sister when any one of these strange men wants to have sex with you, don't fight! You know! Don't make those men angry! Always remember we are just a playground for those boys, let them play, play with them. Don't fight, play, try to make them happy. You know! When they are done playing, they will let you go! And you win! But if you fight them, they fight back, and they will win, and you lose!" It was difficult for Erika just to give up and give in and win, but it worked and knowing that Heidi knew how to deal with men, any number of men, she followed her sister's suggestion. And the evening and night with those Russian soldiers went well, considering the circumstances. The men greatly appreciated Heidi's thoughts and actions. Heidi also talked with the soldiers because she wanted to know what was going on in the world outside the farm. The Russians expected to be in Berlin and finish off Hitler within a week's time. Heidi agreed with the need for the war to end, so they all can go back to living in peace. That group of Russian soldiers left the next day, having gotten what there was to get, food, a hot bath, some rest and the company of two scared women not stupid enough to start a fight with a dozen Russian soldiers.

A week after the Russian soldiers had left, early May 1945; in the morning hours, ten young hoodlums armed with guns surrounded the farmhouse. No shots were fired! The young men searched the farm and were surprised to find no guns, no ammunition, no men, but only two German women. They did not stay long, by mid-afternoon of the same day they had left.

Just ten days later another mob of 15 men arrived. As they were searching the buildings, they realized that only Heidi and Erika were on the farm. The leader of the group assured the two women: “Don’t worry! Nothing will happen to you! We Czech Resistance fighters are chasing down all Nazi war criminals in hiding!” Then one man insisted that Heidi was hiding something under her apron. Two of those nasty beasts undressed and searched Heidi. They found nothing but that she was a pretty good looking woman. One after the other raped Erika's sister. Heidi just let it happen. She even helped one of them undo his pants. Others who had been watching Heidi with keen interest started looking at Erika. Instead of waiting their turn with Heidi, Erika was brutally raped by many of these men too. Time seemed to stand still. That she screamed until she had no voice left was not helping her. Her howling, sobbing, and yowling awakened some sadistic, cruel instincts and increased the interest of several men to torment her some more. Then, before she knew it, the torture was over. The Czech Resistance fighters were done with her and joined those who were waiting to move on. The men left laughing, and Erika listened to two fellows joking with Heidi, telling her "Your friend is a noisy one, but by far not nearly as good as you honey!" As they left, with them went the two motorcycles.

The way Heidi had been holding up seemed to be incredible. Erika had reached the point when she was ready to kill the monsters, knowing that she too would die. But she remembered Heidi's earlier saying: "Don't do them a favor and allow them to kill us! You know! Just think of our parents, brothers, and sister, they want to see us alive when they return home!"

A week went by and another band of criminals disguised as liberation army arrived. They were wearing a variety of uniforms. All of them they had stolen some place. Yes, the last group was worse than the first groups, much worse than any of the Russian soldiers, who all in all, compared to what arrived later, had been true gentlemen. Erika watched much irritated when those thieves slaughtered goats and chickens. But she didn't interfere when being robbed. She knew better than to put up a fight to stop their wants and doings. Erika remembered what Heidi had told her many times, "You fight those bastards, they will kill you! You play their game; they play with you, and you will win in the end because you shall be alive to see the next day!" The latest mob arrived with two vehicles, and they were loading up provisions of meat and baskets filled with potatoes and cabbage. After getting what they came for they left.

In mid-June, after weeks of being left alone, and daily debating to ride on horseback, or use one of their bicycles to visit or not to visit the village, both Heidi and Erika had decided not to leave the Bauernhof. At least here they had a roof over their head and food to eat, and as Erika repeated over and over "We can't just leave! Someone has to make sure we still have a home, a place for our parents, brothers, and sister to return to." Heidi agreed "We need to stay here and keep the farm going. You know!"

The next day another small group of 9 evildoers demanded watches, gold, and whatever may have been hidden. The plunderers, looters, and pillagers had little else in mind aside what to take to make them richer as it pleased them, and nobody was going to stop anyone of them. As three of those men raped Heidi because they felt like it and she fit their idea of amusement. The others searched for valuables. The less they found, the most brutal their threats. And three strong women had joined the group. They were worse than the men, searching all over the place for whatever they could steal, brutal in thought and action. Erika got a beating because she hadn't given them her jewelry. They refused to believe that she had none. Tears were rolling from her eyes as Erika complied and handed them her simple, inexpensive 14kt wedding band after being threatened with death and her finger to be cut off.

After they left, Heidi noticed Erika's bruised arms and legs. Each bruise had a story to tell. Each and every one was evidence of a particular trauma associated with mistreatment and violations she had had to put up with these past months. And again it was Heidi who told Erika "Bringing out the pitchforks and going after those no good bastards, is not helping anyone, we have to be strong. You know! I promise you it will get sooner or later better. I know things will get better!"

Erika and Heidi had experienced the victorious lawless groups of Russian soldiers. Both had been used and abused over and over by unruly Czechs. Undisciplined Slavs and other unscrupulous mixed gangs had left marks on their bodies. What the earlier bands of robbers had not already taken, the latest arriving groups of lawless, loosely organized and badly armed gangs did.

For a few weeks, Erika and Heidi were left alone. No visitors bothered them. Both were worried about not knowing what was going on in the outside world. At some point Heidi offered to visit the village to find out what was happening, to get some new, any news. Again they decided she should not go, the fear of the unknown won. They were going to wait and see. Someone from their family had to come back sooner or later.

In July of 1945, Erika and Heidi were feeding the animals when men in uniforms invaded the farm. They were from two different groups of men who had joined forces. Based on the variety of uniform pants and jackets they wore, it was evident that the uniforms had not been issued to them. Once they were sure that all they were dealing with were two German women, the men were not holding back. They were a very brutal and evil bunch. Some spoke Russian, some Czech, and some Polish. They took whatever they wanted. They also decided to take Erika's sister with them. There were many of them, more than eighteen men! After what Heidi went through with them, she had to wash her messy hair. Barely having rinsed her hair, two guys walked her sister out of the kitchen. Heidi used to laugh a lot, even when there was nothing to laugh about, she did always giggle and giggle she did easily, much too easily. And giggling she was, when the two guys, one to the left and one to the right were saying things to her, which would have made a pig blush.

Erika was unable to help Heidi as they took her. Erika heard her shouting and crying as the two guys handed Heidi to three, four waiting fellows, who just grabbed her, pushed her, and dragged her. They picked her up, carried her, and tossed Heidi like a sack of potatoes onto the bed of a waiting x-German military truck. And a helpless, devastated Erika was forced to watch them leave with her sister Heidi.

It was over a month since Erika's sister had been abducted. Heidi had not returned. The group of those deceptive, atrocious scoundrels had taken her with them. All Erika could do was praying for her sister as she kept herself busy. It was towards the end of August 1945 and Erika was working in the field. The cabbage heads were beautiful and firm, it was time to bring out a sharp knife and cut some off. She filled basket after basket with cabbage, on her own. She used the horse drawn wagon to deliver her harvest to the root cellar. Both her horses were Kladrubers. One was white, one gray. Both very gentle, smart horses. There used to be three Kladrubers in the stables. Schwarzer, the black horse, was Olga's favorite, but neither Olga nor Schwarzer had returned home. The weather was good. There were clouds overhead but no rain. Erika had not heard from anyone, nor seen any person for the past weeks. The only company she had had were her birds, chirping and singing from morning to evening. There was also a pair of crows watching her for hours on some days. Today she was visited by two does. They came right onto the field within a few meters; Erika on her knees between the rows of cabbage talked to those two deer, who seemed to listen. As Erika stood up, scared they ran back up toward the quarry at the foot of the rugged terrain and disappeared behind the hazelnut bushes.

Erika was happy to see three men walking up the road heading to her farm. They did not look threating, no guns, they looked like peaceful regular people. Her hopes for good news were high. She rushed to greet them, and just when she got halfway to them, a truckload of armed volunteers was catching up with the group on foot. Erika didn’t like what she got to hear from that latest group of uninvited guests. Erika had to listen to jokes and laughter: “In town, they are celebrating with hangings of Germans!” “We are beating them to death now!” “The time has come to kick all German ass!” After searching the farm, same as every group of those robbers, thieves and vandals had done before them; one man told Erika: “There is nobody else to be killed here, just you!” Another man told her: “Look at you! Your kind of women, all German whores like you are being sent by trainloads to Siberia and put to work there!” Several men laughed. Some voice let the others know: “No need to murder her. Just take anything whatever you want!”

Erika stood in the barn entrance surrounded by 5 of the men. They pushed her towards and onto a flat-top wooden grain box. With a “How about her?” and the "Komm Frau, that's your lucky day!" Those men put her on top of the bin, and many hands ripped her clothing off. Erika had little choice; she had to endure their doings. As the one or the other man was busy with her, the others gathered what they found useful and loaded it on their truck.

Erika had to listen to one man explain in detail why only very few of the much-hated Nazi Germans died quickly by being shot. “Drowning, being beaten to death, hanged or buried alive, gives them what they deserve. No German life is worth the price of a bullet,” he said. Erika knew better. All of those who terrorized the countryside had guns, but many of them had no ammunition. But in the position, she was in, right there and then, she was not going to say much or even disagree just let things happen. “If nothing else the Frau is sure worth coming here!” didn’t do much for Erika. As they were getting ready to leave, Erika slowly walked over to the house, trying to get cleaned up. She had one of Polish speaking fellows following her. He wanted and got some more, thus as well was not what she wanted. Erika let him do his thing, and she survived. Again Erika was put through great pain and agony. But on the other hand, her latest visitors had left some food for her, and they didn't burn her farm down. A beat-up Erika was happy to see those visitors leaving because all they had been was shocking bad news. She realized, she still had shelter and hope she had too. And since she had still some remaining chicken fat she was able to treat her soreness due to abrasions in both the vaginal and rectal areas as well.

In late September, it looked like rain but was already cold enough to snow. For about a month, Erika had been alone, with no interruptions. She was digging up and harvesting potatoes. When the next horde of young men arrived and announced, "Frau, your neighbor kaput!" Erika had already seen smoke rising from over the hill, even before they told her that they had set fire to the Bartsch farm.

Imagine her surprise to hear that these villains had been forced to kill her neighbor because he had attacked two of the young hooligans with a large sharp sword. Erika offered to clean the boys ugly looking open wounds. One young man had a shoulder injury, the other a deep cut on his arm, right through to the bone.

She put an herbal mixture of thistle and oak bark on the wounds, and she used clean cotton strips to bandage the guys. Then she made an herbal tea to help them relax and sleep. While doing so, she found out that those boys had not planned to kill anyone when they came looking for Nazis on the Bartsch property. The scoundrels told Erika that her neighbor had started a fight, all because that German fellow's wife was going crazy. The young man with the shoulder wound told Erika "She spoke fluent Czech and told us they are a Czech family. We knew better. First, she was silly, erratic, loony too." Pointing at the other fellow with the cut in his arm, "When Hanuš grabbed her, he came out with his sword, the German fellow. Told us in German, to let go of her. We knew she lied." And the one by the name of Hanuš confirmed "Glad the Nazi is dead. The woman was kooky, really wacky!" as the first attested to what Hanuš had said, "They all, the whole family was preposterous, wild and screwy." Hanuš sounded disappointed when he let Erika know "Lubomir, and me didn't get involved with the women. We helped each other to stop the bleeding."

Again and again, Erika followed orders of whatever evil-minded nationals, asked her to do. She knew that she was their property as long as they called her farm theirs, as long as they stayed. That gang of criminals left early the next day. They had more important things to do than bother with poor Erika. In return, she changed the bandages for the two youngsters. These boys were not even twenty years old. The wounds looked already better. Erika was sure they would recover if they kept the cuts clean. She mentioned to the one with the shoulder cut: "There is a doctor in the village. Have the doctor put a couple of stitches in it! It will help it to heal faster and better." Helpless Erika watched as they stole her two Kladrubers for those two wounded guys to ride on.

Soon after they had left without killing her or burning her farm down, Erika climbed the path along the hill behind her farm and over the forested ridge to check on her neighbors. Sliding more than walking downhill, she went to see the Bartsch property. Smoke was still rising, here and there, small fires were smoldering. The solid stone and mortar walls of the main house were still standing. Only the roof had collapsed. Both the barn and stable had burned to the ground.

Ralf Bartsch's headless corpse was outside the main house. His clothes showed burn marks and bullet holes. When Erika discovered his wife's lifeless naked body, the broken wine bottles, and saw how they had used the same on Frau Bartsch, she got sick. It was Erika who took her apron off and covered the dead woman's body, as good as she could. Erika said her prayers. Realizing there was nothing she could do for them now, Erika turned around and started to go back up the path to the top of the hill. That's when she saw them. On Erika's left side, in the entrance to Bartsch family's root cellar, the one dug into the mountainside, she noticed two naked feet. Expecting the very worst she stumbled off her path through the bushes to the rock entrance of the cellar. What she saw made Erika faint. She had to throw up! And it took some time to gather her strength and be on her way back home. Had she known that before, she would have put poison into the wounds of those boys last night. She could have poisoned their food; those young men deserved to die like rats. But maybe it was not their doing? But who else was responsible for the heinous killing and dismemberment of those two young girls?

From the ridge she looked back, grateful to be alive. After one more prayer, slowly, slipping and sliding, she made it down the hill to her family's farm. Erika had to stop several times blinded by her tears. She couldn't stop crying. She had to pause, drained of all energy Erika sat down between the blueberry bushes. Leaning against a tree stump, Erika was asking the question: "God why is this all happening. Have all men gone crazy?" And she was looking up at the clouds above and praying for all those who by no fault of their own had been hurt in wars. And she wished real hard that those Russian soldiers had been able to find him the person responsible for the war and all the associated suffering. As she looked to the heavens for an answer to her prayers, big snowflakes floated gently by her face. The first snow was falling, and, ever so slowly, it added a carpet of white, covering the blood stained soil.

It was already the third week of autumn. As the leaves changed colors, the days were getting shorter, and the weather changed too. Sitting by the window, Erika sat by the window, knitting. She hadn't made a baby dress since several years ago. The first snow two weeks earlier didn't stick around, but there was more to come soon. She listened to the wind, to the tap-tap of water drops. Her thoughts were with her family, wishing they are well, and to be unharmed. She was telling herself that she had no control over her parents, brothers, sisters and her husband's life. They all were in God's hands. Her job was to take care of herself, and the new life within, just because!

Erika was longing for any news from Helmut, waiting for her husband to come back home from the war. She was desperate for news, any news. It was six months now since the first group of Russians had visited her farm. She was waiting to hear from Olga, her younger sister, as she was waiting for a word from Hans and Fritz, her two brothers who were soldiers in the German Wehrmacht. Erika also had not heard a word from Lorenz and Marta, her parents, who went to visit Prague and had not returned. About Heidi, somehow Erika knew Heidi could handle any situation. Still, Erika prayed daily for Heidi, her older sister, who had left, this summer, and not by her choice! A horde of thugs had schlepped her away. It was much more tormenting to worry about her family members than her bodily pain. Erika's blue and red marks on legs and arms and body, the reminders from being grabbed and held, banged and pushed were slowly fading.

Yes! Since July, when her older sister had been dragged away, no one but Erika was on the farm. Erika was born on the farm and had always lived on the farm. She had worked the land all her life. Aside from going to church a few times a year, she had always stayed home. Farming and taking care of the animals was her life. True she had not been doing too well in school, never made it past the 4th grade, but when it came to farming, nobody in her family knew more than her.

Just before leaving for Prague, Marta and Lorenz had been talking about handing the Bauer farm over to their oldest son, upon his return from the military, just as it had been the custom for generations. Erika's Helmut had inherited a large acreage and farm from his parents. She knew quite well that much work was waiting for them as soon as he was coming back home to her. It was part of her parents' plan to see Erika having a happy life with her husband on his farm.

That winter she felt lonely at times. It had never been more important for her to take care of the farm, and not abandon it. Erika was expecting her family members to come back home. She was going to make sure they all had a home waiting for them.

Life was no longer what it once had been. She felt under the weather, some days sick, exhausted she rested on her bed. But she had to stay strong. Erika knew the bruises would go away. She had decided to be grateful for being alive. She still had all limbs, and no bones in her body had been broken. Erika trusted in a Divine Power that all her suffering would soon be over, and order return. She knew why she was feeling different. Her breasts had been getting bigger.

Erika had not had her period for several months now. She had been gaining weight. Erika was getting used to the fact that she was pregnant.

Winter had put all outside activities on hold. More than one meter of snow covered the dirt road to her farm. It kept all visitors out. The broad-leaved hardwood trees had lost their leaves. Here and there naked tree branches were layered with snow. The pine trees were snow laden. Ice and snow partially covered the creek below, yet she could hear it whispering and splashing as it made its way over the rocks. Without interruption from the outside world, Erika had plenty to do, all day long. She got up at dawn; she had to feed her animals, to clean up after them, to gather eggs, and to milk the cows. Erika was grateful for having enough food to eat. Erika stayed busy. One day she was baking bread. The next day she was cutting cabbage, she had brought in from the root cellar, to be fermented in a big barrel, as she was making Sauerkraut. And she also made cheese from the cream she had separated from the milk.

Erika was knitting. She was glad that she had a trunk full of knitting yarn. It belonged to Marta, her mother. Father had bought it for his wife because her mother had promised to knit a sweater for every member of the family for Christmas. Christmas 1945 came, and New Year 1946 arrived. Erika knitted baby clothing from the yarn. She made hats, pants, socks, sweaters, and dresses.

As she took inventory, from the one dozen pigs, only two were left. A handful of hens and a rooster had gotten away and had been living in the nearby bushes. However, they had come home at the first snowfall. Her unwanted houseguests had consumed the rest of the chickens. And there was not one left of her herd of goats. Erika was glad she still had the two old cows for milk. The last bunch of hoodlums and murderers had also taken her two horses. “How am I going to plow the fields in the spring?” She asked herself thinking about the springtime, which always follows the winter.

Then there were those days when she was thinking of leaving after the snow melts! But where else could she go? Where to could she go? Go and get murdered in town? And she decided: “If so, to die on home soil is surely a better choice." She had heard enough about what was happening in the villages and seen on the neighbor's farm. No! She was not going to leave. Erika had decided: "I stay, and leave it all in God's hands!"

With the arrival of spring, the snow started to melt. A Czech Official arrived in a military-all-wheel-drive. He happened not only to be a friend of her family, he Pana Primátor was the grandfather of the Bartsch kids. He explained to her that he was appointed to oversee all German owned land in the area, including the Bauer Bauernhof. During his visit, he made it quite clear to her: "As part of the ongoing expulsion of Germans, all of the Bauer property has been confiscated and will be handed over to new owners within the month." When Erika puzzled looked at him and asked: "What about me?" He assured her "Yes, Frau Bauer, I meant to say Frau Franken, you are allowed to stay until the arrival of the new Czech owners." The Czech Official did promise that he would try to put the Bauer farm in real good hands. He had plans to give it to a close relative, a cousin of his wife. He also promised to do whatever he can so she wouldn't be harmed other than the loss of property. Somehow Erika felt relieved. When they talked about the Bartsch family, he knew about the slaughter of his daughter and the two girls, as well as the husband. "It was a shocking experience to see such senseless, cruel actions!" he said with teary eyes.

Then when he said "Thank you for covering her with your apron!" he had tears running from his eyes. Erika didn't know how he knew, and what to say until he added: "I recognized your *EBr* monogram!" And Erika couldn't help it. She was crying hard. They were now both sobbing, and he put his arm around her not saying a word, but she knew, he knew how disappointed she was with the world around her.

When her tears ebbed, and she looked at her apron, she realized that yes she had not yet changed it to her new name. She also hadn't bought anything new lately, and as it was the custom, she always added a decorative *EBr* to identify her personal possessions.

Erika with a demanding voice said to Pana Primátor: "Can you please make sure that the crime which happened to those poor girls and the Bartsch family doesn't get unpunished!

What these beasts did it's unbelievable. These two kids didn't do any harm to anyone!" He answered her, "If I can, I shall, however Frau Franken look here," and he showed her a piece of paper and read it to her: *"Any act committed between September 1938 and October 28, 1945, the object of which was to aid the struggle for liberty of the Czechs and Slovaks or which represented just reprisals for actions of the occupation forces and their accomplices, is not illegal, even when such acts may otherwise be punishable by law. This law does de facto ensure that no atrocities against Germans during such time period in question will ever be prosecuted in Czechoslovakia."* And he put the paper away from where he had read and looked in Erika's teary eyes. He did say: "I am sorry Frau Franken, it is not right, I know! It's just not right!"

"Is there a way to chase down those murderers of the Bartsch family?" She asked. "It's most unlikely! Most unlikely. Believe me! I want them all dead too!" He said holding the hand of the sobbing, crying, Erika.

Two weeks later, a Czech family arrived and took over the Bauer farm. Erika told the new Czech owner and his wife that she was with child and she had no place to go. They were good people. They had already decided to let her stay on as their maid, and as promised by the Czech Official Pana Primátor they were prepared to protect Erika as good as possible from any harm. Erika was feeling a lot safer than her alone in charge of the farm with all those dirty, smelly lewd men running lose, and being all over and after her.

On the farm, she gave birth to a baby girl in the spring of 1946, and both had food and shelter. Erika was happy, as happy as anyone can be. The maid job guaranteed food for her and the baby. And they had a safe place to live. Sleeping in the barn was much better than being out in the cold. Erika worked with and for the new owners. She did as told because she didn't want to be sent away. Erika took good care of her baby. She carried her girl with her, wherever she went.

End of 1947, Erika got news that Helmut would never come back, her husband had been declared fallen near Leningrad, in January of 1944, lost mail, stating the facts, finally arrived, years later. "What now, what was there to look forward to?" A devastated Erika asked herself.

When Erika thought things couldn't get any worse, it did. All she was used to, the living on the Bauer Bauernhof, the guarantee to have food, a roof over her head, and to have work she enjoyed while raising a daughter, ended with a political decision, the expulsion of all Sudeten Germans. It was in December of 1948 that she was told: "Erika as part of the law, which requires the 'Expulsion of all Sudeten Germans,' you too are to be deported, you need to leave!" And the Czech family she was living with and working for expressed their disbelief in the countries politicians, to be so cruel, not understanding the common people. They also didn't understand the deep hatred which had grown to such a point.

Neither the Czech family nor Erika would have believed it, but still 65 years later in May 2013 the Czech president, Mr. Zeman told Austrian reporters that *...the so-called Sudeten*

Germans, or former Czechoslovakia's three-million-strong ethnic German minority, should have been happy to be merely expelled from their homeland in the wake of the second world war.

"When a citizen of some country collaborates with a country that has occupied his state, an expulsion is a subtler [form of] punishment than, for example, a death penalty," he told a news agency!"

As it was getting closer to the day of Erika's leaving, the Czech family she had been working for and with since the spring of 1946, they warned her over and over, "Erika you must take the train to the Western Zone. Do not get on any train to the Russian Zone!" But Erika had no idea, why the Western Zone would be better than the Russian Zone, both meant leaving what she knew as her home. Still, because she believed that the Czech couple had only her best interest in mind, she was telling herself "Take Western Zone train!" and "Take Western Zone train!"

In March of 1949, Erika joined a group of German deportees marching several kilometers to the train station in deep snow. Some older people were not able to walk. Armed volunteers were there and made sure that everyone followed their deportation orders. They all had bayonets on their rifles. Those who couldn't walk were exposed to die a horrible death, at some places along the path frozen corpses told their story. Erika was carrying her girl on her back. In her hand, she held a small bundle with half a loaf of bread, a bottle of milk and a few necessities. She walked as if their life depended on it, and it did.

At the train station entrance, the deportees had to pass through a gate. Here, armed men, some in uniform, some not, checked each "Aussiedler" one by one. Every deportee got padded down, before being herded to a waiting train. Some were ordered to step aside, only to be searched more thoroughly. And Erika got to see how those armed thieves were pocketing items; they stole watches, jewelry, and anything valuable to them before letting those to be deported go any further. Erika watched as four young women, one by one were selected and separated from the group. Several soldiers escorted them to the station buildings. She saw three women being herded to the main door of the station, the forth by herself was directed to a side door.

Then it was Erika's turn. After taking a sip from a metal flask to keep warm, a short fat civilian man motioned Erika to follow him. When she didn't do so right away, hands pushed her. "Jit! Go! Frau! Komm! Now! Go!" Two soldiers in uniform encouraged her to hurry up "Jit! Komm! Go!" They pointed the way to a door next to the side door; the one she had seen the other woman go in. The room she was taken to, it was empty except a big desk and one chair. Here now one of the three men escorting Erika took her Frieda away, another checked her bundle for contrabands. Erika heard voices from the next room. The dividing door between the rooms was wide open. She heard a male voice shouting: "Alles ausziehen, mach schon!" and some female crying: "...ist doch zu kalt hier!" Erika was told the same, she too was ordered to undress. It was cold in the room. She watched the soldiers as they searched her clothing, and as told she took off her clothing piece by piece. Erika was wearing many layers because of the cold. She heard the voices in the next room, and it sounded like someone was beating the woman next door because she wasn't following orders. Erika heard the woman's voice, as she was begging, sobbing and promising to do whatever, anything.

No! Erika was going to follow orders, and she was not afraid of being naked. She was not going to defend herself when she was called a mature well-fed Nazi-swine and a “devka.” That one stocky, short fat fellow about Erika's size, who had been giving Erika orders, made her shudder. In his voice was beguilement, but his actions were wicked "...a well-fed pig..." he said kneading her belly from the navel down. Then squeezing her breast "...feel those baggies..." he encouraged the other men to do like him. Then as she stepped out of her undergarments, he was squeezing her butt cheeks: "a lot of Schinken, firm...!"

Erika shivered as she stood there in only her underskirt when the man pushed her back onto the desk. His foul breath reeked of tobacco and alcohol. His enormous, rough, work hardened hands grabbed her by the knees, and with an “Oh have a good look at those ham hocks!" he forced her legs wide apart. It was cold in the room. Freezing on the outside, cold within, mixed with fear caused her to shiver. That man now standing between her knees was taking credit by announcing: "...vidět, look the svine is vibrating, she wants Jarek!"

Erika got to listen to the "Yes Jarek! You picked out a mature, healthy robust, firm one! Not like yesterday, the dried up, bony, cold and useless, Nazi whore!" Erika heard one fellow praising her as by far the best choice all week. She didn't like the hands on her knees, or those other hands, some guy fingering her, or the man who was stroking her breast, one by one like he was trying to milk her. Erika gathered that these guys' daily entertainment, and to kill time, consisted of gang raping helpless women.

Always having had food to eat, Erika looked so much healthier and therefore more attractive than most other German women these days. A good number of the women she had walked with to the train were just skin and bones, and some were very sick. Erika, having an idea what was coming next, tried everything she could do, not to scare her little girl. She begged the stocky fellow in front of her, now undoing his belt, to do, as he wants but please-please not to frighten her little girl, her Frieda.

A new face stepped next to Jarek, a tall young man in his early twenties, in a brand-new looking uniform. Erika felt hypnotized by his bright green eyes. He was pushing forward past Jarek, and because he hadn't been there all week, he asked: "Wasn't I supposed to do this one first?" Nobody disagreed, including Jarek who showed respect by saluting and mumbled: “Yes, Walter we picked the Frau for your initiation, as a special treat for our good friend from Moskau!”

If the circumstances were different, the soldier with the green eyes, Erika didn't mind. He was somehow different, not like his friends. He had some aura to him. He had manners. More, however, Erika was not afraid of him mistreating her. With less mixed feelings, hypnotized by the unusual bright green eyes, Erika surrendered to him. The green-eyed fellow was gentle, firm, and dissimilar from all the other men who had had their way with her. Those others were getting their kicks out of hurting her, violating her body was not enough for them, grabbing and squeezing and beating pleased them. With the green-eyed soldier, Erika felt very relaxed as her body welcomed his manhood and reacted with an orgasm while being impregnated by him. Erika was in a state of amazement. It had never happened to her before, the jolt, the spasm, the feeling of awe about her body's reaction. Heidi had been bragging about her having all kinds of them, any place, any man. For Erika, it was a moment of feeling permissive. Nevertheless, it didn't last.

To be gentle was not true for those after him. It started with Jarek. He seemed to thrive on having her wiggle, squirm, and bounce. Jarek didn't mind to hurt her, to make her shake and quake, he did so on purpose. Erika complied; she knew she had no choice. Spread out on the desk Erika heard Frieda's voice, as she was crying. She wanted to be held by her mother. But Erika was unable to get out of the grip of the hands that held her in place on the desk. Jarek called Erika: "Luscious piece of meat!" Another man, who had just arrived, was bragging about the woman he had picked out the other week: "She was hot, from every angle, from every side, she was a fine find, wasn't she? She was young and wasn't she a juicy one too!" Somebody said: “That píča! She took the Russia train!”

Erika tried to block out everything, to shut down her feelings, and not hear the men’s lewd comments. She didn’t want to listen any of the coarse and vulgar suggestions made for the sake of the men’s amusement and additional entertainment. Erika just wanted them to climb on, climb off, be done, and let her go! And somehow she recalled Heidi, talking about a similar situation, she had been telling her: “Erika we are just a playground for those boys, we let them play, and play with them. You can’t win a fight. So play, when they are done playing they will let you go!” And that's what Erika did; she didn’t put up any resistance.

Erika listened to the door opening and slamming shut several times. Men were leaving, more men coming. And at some point, her hair had become undone, had dropped to the floor. Hands squeezed her breast, maybe the same who was also stepping on her hair! Erika heard her Frieda voice and crying she was a lot. She knew she had to hang on, play their game. Erika was telling herself: "You have been through worse, in the months just after the war.” The men cheered "Stephan...! Stephan....! Stephan...! Stephan...!" And he was doing his darnedest by banging and beating on her, until he was done, and softened up. Then it was bad breath Jarek again, who penetrated her.

A loud voice announced that hands were needed, to restrain two Nazi women next door. Someone mentioned that they had caught those two with gold and lots of jewels. Jarek who had barely started, now suddenly withdrew. Jarek was ordering Erika "Stay here! Frau you not move!" pulling his pants up he followed the others!

All the men had left to see those two women next door, only one remained, the green-eyed soldier. With a caring, friendly voice he urged her: "Get up Frau." And he helped her up, apologizing he picked up Frieda as he said: "Here! Please! Go now! Hurry up! Your train is going!"

Hastily Erika dressed. With no time to put on her undergarments, she grabbed Frieda, who had stopped crying, from the stranger's arms.

Erika looked for the galoshes she had worn earlier but couldn't find them. Erika heard a woman's hysterical scream coming from next door. "Take your dirty hands off my sister's ass! Du Drecksau! Du!" Another woman's voice was yelling at someone: "Nein, not that way!" A man's voice was ordering both women to shut up. Another told Jarek to go ahead and check for hidden valuables in both women's orifices now.

The first female voice loud and clear disagreed with being searched. The same voice insisted: "...you already got all and everything that we had sewn into our undergarments." She was asked to stop kicking. And whatever she did, she was asked not to try it again. A laughing male voice suggested, "Let me take care of her!" Erika heard a woman's "Now go to hell!" accompanied by a slapping sound.

Next, there was a plop, plop, and there was silence, death silence.

Erika stopped looking for her galoshes; she just ran, and she ran for her life. For the sake of her daughter, Erika had to get to the West. Erika, barefoot, carrying a scared Frieda in her arms, ran as fast as she could out to the train, which was just about to depart. Helping hands reached out, grabbed hold of Frieda. More hands held onto Erika's arms and lifted both up into the freight car. Exhausted she fell and rolled across the floor, Frieda close to her. She broke down, and cried, and wept. Someone handed her some rags, and someone else wrapped them around her blue feet. It felt good to feel the tickling as the blood circulated again. Feeling the train moving, Erika prayed, she was thanking God for being allowed to leave.

The train took Erika to the West, to Bavaria, to the American Zone. That last shameful experience didn't matter to Erika. She had been through worse. It may, however, have done something to Frieda, who since as a child, was scared of being touched by men.

Were those war crimes against the German civilian population an exception at the end of the war? Did it only happen in the Sudetenland? No, by no means, not at all! The truth is that it happened throughout the war-torn territory once called the Reich.

What is worse is that little has changed by today on our planet and that war crimes still happen, regardless of news coverage and the world knows about those occurrences.

After WW II, were German women spared because they obviously were not Nazis or involved in warfare whatsoever? Well, not really, according to the reports Sepp had read: “In Neisse, Silesia, 182 Catholic nuns were reported having been raped. In the diocese of Kattowitz, 66 pregnant nuns were counted. In one convent when the older Mother Superior and her assistant tried to protect the younger nuns with outstretched arms, they were killed.” A priest reported in the Nord Amerika magazine for November 1, 1945, that he knew "several villages where all the women, even the aged and girls as young as twelve were violated daily for weeks by the victorious army!"

As Erika arrived at the train station at the Refugee camp near Ansbach, Northern Bavaria, in the American Zone, she was desperate. She needed some shoes to cover her feet. True, she had not had any decent shoes since months before she had gladly accepted to be the maid on her family farm. One of her uninvited guests had taken her last pair of good shoes. From the farm to the train station she had worn a much too big pair of old galoshes, the kind she used to wear for field-work and to clean stables. Rushing to the train, she had left them behind in the train station office, as well as her long underwear and their food bundle.

Erika, like many others, all she had was what she wore now and a little girl, her daughter Frieda. Getting off the train, nearly missing a step, that's when she slipped, stumbled and landed on him, the tall man standing and looking for someone, but not for her. She didn't know that the man was a shoemaker, and didn't have any idea that he too was from the Sudetenland, and it was only later in the day that he told her his name, Waldemar Schuster.

Waldemar Schuster had been in Ansbach already for close to four years. He still waited for news, any news from his family, from his friends and his workers back home in the Sudetenland, all to no avail. By now Waldemar had his small shoemaker shop in the Lager. He also worked two days a week for the same shoemaker he had started out with in Ansbach. Waldemar had been able to obtain by buying, bartering and trading, all the needed tools of the trade, including several sets of pairs of wooden lasts, and a Singer Sewing Machine.

Waldemar's philosophy as to making an existence was strictly one of "Rich is who is able bodied to work! Therefore you work, you eat, you live, you do good work, and you live good!"

Here in Ansbach Waldemar had occasionally been visiting with the one or the other lonely woman for a glass of wine, a dinner together, and having a casual sexual affair here and there as well. Waldemar was too busy and not interested in any meaningful liaison, and he had unquestionably no plans to get married again.

Then at the end of March 1949, the woman at the train station with no shoes and the little girl fell into his arms. Waldemar had met every train from the Sudetenland over the past four years in Ansbach. He still had some hopes that members of his family or some friends may be on the transport from the East. He was looking for any of the "Aussiedlers" (deportees) from home, anyone he may know.

Again there were no familiar faces amidst the arrivals. That's when the woman with the little girl fell on him. Holding her before she fell to the ground he somewhat angry asked "Kannste nich aufpassen? Can't you watch your step?" When he looked at her bare feet, scratched, with blueish discoloring of cold burns, tenderheartedness took over. He had a pair of shoes in his rucksack. Half boots he had planned to deliver to a storekeeper not far from the station. They were men's ankle boots, but they had to do it until they got to his shop. Erika followed him in shoes much too big for her, beholden to have her feet protected against the cold.

Waldemar Schuster was a trained professional maker of shoes. During his apprenticeship as a cobbler in 1905 through 1909 in Troppau, shoes were still made by hand, one at the time. He knew how to make fitting shoes for the feet that demanded protection, one pair at a time, and all by hand. And knowing how to make new shoes, made repairing of used shoes an easy task.

Waldemar, now age 59, found some shoes for Erika, then 46 years young, and fitted them for her feet. As she had not had any proper fitting shoes to wear, for many years, Erika was the happiest she had been in a very-very long time. Waldemar also made boots for Erika's daughter Frieda. Any time he touched the little girl, she cried and tried to run away. It was still winter, and the right shoes made all the difference when trying to walk around in the snow and dirt. In the end, Waldemar won, and Frieda ended up with a nice pair of boots. Knowing that being grateful requires some action; Erika cooked for Waldemar and stayed with him until she was relocated by the authorities to another refugee camp near Kitzingen.

About nine months after Erika had her shoes fitted by Waldemar, Sepp was born. Erika put on Sepp's birth certificate Sepp Bauer, using her maiden name. She had not seen Waldemar since she had left the refugee camp in Ansbach. She had sent him a letter, but because of her limited ability to write, the letter must have gone lost.

Nevertheless, it happened, as it had to happen that Waldemar was asked to relocate to Kleinerort, and on his way there he needed some papers signed in Kitzingen. As he was getting his paperwork for Kleinerort in order, Erika walked into the same office with Frieda on one hand and in the other hand a woven container. Looking at the little bundle in the basket Waldemar asked "And who is that!" and she answered, "It's our son, Sepp!" Erika was so grateful not only to run into Waldemar but that he was there to help her filling out all the papers where she had been unable to write some words readable. That's why she was asked to return to the office in the first place. Yes she could read letter-by-letter, word-by-word slowly, and yes she could write but just didn't know what letters to use for some of those words, and some letters of the alphabet she wrote backward, whereby she had no problems to pronounce them when speaking.

Waldemar saddened about his losses because of the war, was looking at the woman in front of him. Her hands full with those two little ones, and she was happy, overjoyed to see someone she knew, someone who had helped her when she had no shoes. He was aware that she looked up to him because he was so calm amidst the tragedies around them. "About the boy! Was it his? Most likely!" Waldemar was thinking, and he knew: "I don't have much to share, all my highly valued, prized possessions, my wife, the house, the shop, family properties, they are all gone by now! But, I still have hands and skills and the ability to feed a family." And barely finishing his thoughts, loud he said: "Erika you, Frieda and Sepp all come with me!"

Soon after, Waldemar married Erika, as it was the right thing to do. And Erika Schuster moved with her husband Waldemar to Kleinerort. And Sepp Bauer became Sepp Schuster.

What was growing up in the American Zone like after WW II? All Sepp Schuster learned about the end of the war in the years to come, was by reading and listening to adults talking about the 'Heimat.' The fall of Berlin was not the end, it turned out to be the beginning, a new start, and sometimes it was as brutal as the war and as rocky as life can be.

One of the greatest crimes against women in all of history surely should be in the Guinness book of world records namely: “The number of women raped at the end of WWII in what used to be Deutsches Reich!” As we know only too well, and sometimes we don't want to be reminded of it: ‘The culprits were obviously Red Army soldiers and some of them from the Far East and Central Asian Republics of the Soviet Union. Let us not forget there were also the American, the French and British soldiers.’ The American soldiers didn’t have to use much force to have sex with German or Austrian girls and women. These Fräuleins had no illusions, they had experienced the raw brutalities of war, had been running for shelter as bombs rained down on them, and each of them knew ‘death’ because they had buried loved ones. In the American zone, German women had more of a freedom of choice than in the other zones, notably the Russian region. Almost all the young American soldiers in Germany and Austria; they were having a real good time. For the young men in uniform, the getting a date in Germany was much easier compared to at home. They had no problem to figure out how to make those Fräuleins do things, anything. The American soldiers offered the girls hope. They gave them presents! And those young men made the Fräuleins laugh and crying tears of joy and had them dance and be happy. They drank with them and slept with them. The Fräuleins were ready to be cheered up. To enjoy the gifts as offered by the winning side was the only right answer.

The Christian Century for December 5, 1945, reported: *"the American provost marshal, Lieutenant Colonel Gerald F. Beane, said that rape presents no problem for the military police because a bit of food, a bar of chocolate, or a bar of soap seem to make rape unnecessary."*

The Weekly Review of London, for October 25, 1945, described it thus: *"Young girls, unattached, wander about and freely offer themselves for food or bed ... very simply, they have one thing left to sell, and they sell it ... as a way of dying it may be worse than starvation, but it will put off dying for months -- or even years."*

Then there was the Marshall plan, and what had looked quite bleak, started to look rosier, day-by-day. And Germany got a new currency starting with 20 Deutsche Marks, per person, much money to spend in 1949 - 1950. It did replace the barter system, which had been widely in use, aside from the American Cigarette currency.

What was the real number of refugees after WW II? Who knows? After WW II West Germany alone took in more than 14 million German deportees and refugees who needed a new place to live. Every village was asked to take in some of the refugees, to provide a place to live for those Germans without a home. Kleinerort had asked for one family only, and they preferred a trained craftsman like a carpenter, barrel maker, mechanic or shoemaker. They got a shoemaker. Kleinerort got Waldemar Schuster and his family.

In 1951 Waldemar Schuster was assigned to Kleinerort, a small village located in a valley, in the middle of the Steigerwald, being part of the Frankenland, located in northern Bavaria. How about the meaning of Frankenland? The origin of the word ‘Frank’ is known to be ‘free,' and the Schuster family enjoyed their freedom to have a place they could call home and an opportunity to start over.

The roads to and from Kleinerort were all dirt and gravel roads. The street through the village itself was paved. An ancient cobblestone pavement separated the south from the north side, and all homes were located side-by-side facing the one and only thoroughfare. There were 12 buildings on each side of the road, all old buildings. 17 of the 24 buildings lining the street had towards the back a farm and a slice of farmland belonging to each farmstead. The earliest settlement in Kleinerort dated back to the 7th century, but was burned down around Napoleon’s time, and rebuilt shortly after. That was the Schaeferhof and farm.

On the west-end was Kleinerort's only store, a general store owned by the Kaufmann family. They carried candy, glass bottles and jars, a very limited assortment of housewares and kitchen items. They sold soaps, oils, and candles. The Kaufmann’s kept needles, cotton and some fabrics in stock, and were willing to order and get whatever may be available from the reps and salesmen who visited Kleinerort periodically.

Smack in the middle of the south side was the 'Gasthaus Zum Lamm' and behind it was the local brewery. Herr Braumeister managed the brewery and his brother owned and operated the 'Gasthaus Zum Lamm.' The beer brewed at the 'Zum Lamm Brewery' was still made from the four original ingredients, in compliance with the 1516 Bavarian law and the Reinheitsgebot, nothing but water, malted barley, hops, and yeast went in to the making for the local beer.

Across the street from the 'Gasthaus Zum Lamm' was the 'Gasthaus Zur Sonne.' In the building attached to the same was the local bakery. Every family in Kleinerort got their bread from 'Anita & Anna's Bakery' a mother and daughter team. Anita, the mother, was known to bake the best Brezels (pretzel) and Broetchen (rolls) any place near Kleinerort. Sepp never had equally good or better Brezels anyplace. The mother's Brezel and Broetchen were mainly for the 'Gasthaus Zum Lamm' and 'Gasthaus Zur Sonne,' and as preordered. Anna also baked cakes for special occasions. She made and decorated cakes to order for birthdays, holidays, and what have you. Wedding cakes were Anna's specialty. She was not married yet and already in her late thirties. Her mother was married. Anita's husband Herr Wirt was the owner of the 'Gasthaus Zur Sonne.'

To the west side of the 'Gasthaus Zur Sonne,' next to the bakery was a small open space, a gathering place for the villagers and the schoolhouse. The building used to house the church, when Kleinerort was still Catholic, at some time before 1700. The old large 2-story school building with a clock tower was built from massive sandstone blocks, with walls made to withstand the time. Herr Hauptlehrer Meyer and his wife lived upstairs. Downstairs were the classroom and several storage rooms.

Kleinerort was surrounded by gentle hills topped with leftovers from the Middle-Ages, old castles, ruins, all reminders of a different era, and plenty of woodlands. Extensive forests covered most of the hillsides. Certain areas consisted of planted conifers; the rest were deciduous trees.

Here Waldemar and Erika and kids were provided with a two-room sandstone building, which had been empty and not heated for a very long time. The walls were damp; the place was dark and cold. Only the front room had a stove and served as well as the kitchen. That was Waldemar's workshop. The back room barely was big enough for two beds. Behind the building were the outhouse and a rusty-old-well-hand-pump. The water was good, it had a hint of sour to it, and Waldemar said: "It's good and healthy water." There was also a long narrow plot of land behind the building, with more than a dozen fruit trees. Erika was however told that those fruit trees belonged to the Denninger family, and therefore she needed the owner's permission to pick any of the fruit.

Erika and Waldemar did their best to raise their son Sepp and his sister Frieda in their small, damp quarters on the west end of Kleinerort opposite the grocery store. Erika was helping the farmers in the fields. She dragged Frieda along while carrying Sepp on her back. She couldn't leave those kids with Waldemar as he had his hands full with repairing all kind of leather harnesses aside from those shoe repairs.

Six months had passed. Waldemar went to talk to Kleinerort's mayor: "Herr Buergermeister we need to look for another place with more comfortable living conditions. The place is cold. The kids are sick all the time. It is not working for us. I was thinking about going back to Ansbach, and work for the same shop I used to work at, just to have a dry and more comfortable place to live!"

"But we need you here; the small house is all we had sitting empty!" Herr Buergermeister answered. And Waldemar said: "Then give me a piece of land. And I build my very own place."

By now the folks in Kleinerort were used to have a cobbler, and instead of having to travel 22 kilometers to the next shoemaker shop Waldemar got his wish granted. The village leased Waldemar a plot of land outside the village, just below the dump. Using resources provided by the government such as "Lastenausgleich" money given to help rebuild the country. Waldemar built the 'Häusle' (little home) with the aid of several villagers and using wood provided by a nearby lumber mill. Out-front a well got drilled, and within six months the Schuster family moved in.

Their 'Häusle' had a kitchen, living room, one large bedroom for Erika and the kids, big enough for three beds, and a smaller room for Waldemar as his room and shop. They also had an outhouse behind the house, next to a storage shed, where Erika kept her garden tools. The following year in the spring, Waldemar added a much-needed separate shoemaker shop to it, he built it using concrete blocks. It was attached to the original 'Häusle.' At the same time, he also added a small barn for Erika, to store hay, space for her rabbits and chicken, as well as the goats during the winter months. And he connected the home and the barn with an enclosed walkway, which allowed for additional storage, and provided an enclosed and covered area, for the pump, and anything that needed to be stored and to be readily available like the 2 Zuendapp Mopeds and Waldemar's bike.

It took two years, but by then Waldemar had gotten what he wanted, his very own space, and a clean, dry place to live. Here Erika had plenty of space to grow what she needed on vegetables for the family. And there was plenty of room for Sepp to run around too. By now Frieda was going to school, and after school, she went to help Erika in the fields unless she had homework to do. Erika preferred to have both kids with her because Waldemar was always busy fixing what needed to be fixed. There was plenty of work to be done for the villagers; much of it was fasten, stitching and sewing by hand. In those first three years in Kleinerort, Waldemar didn't get to make any new shoes, but he repaired a lot of worn out shoes and boots, as well as other leather items.

Looking back, Sepp kindly remembered those times that Waldemar had him sitting on his lap and was reading to him from Frieda's school-books. His father also showed Sepp the letters of the ABC, and he taught him to count by having Sepp adding and subtracting nails from a box of 20 which Waldemar expanded to a box of 100. There was much that little Sepp learned from his father.

As Sepp was growing up, he played with other village boys, whenever he could. Sepp didn't know what was happening, every so often when he played with other kids on the street, or in the fields behind the homes, the parents of the same called their children back into the house. And Sepp was left playing by himself.

One day a village boy, same age as Sepp, hit Sepp's head with a hammer while the two were playing in a sand pile on the side of the road. It hurt, and there was some blood in his hair. Wanting to know why the boy hit him he asked, "Ja! What for? Why you hit me?" He admitted that because his parents had told him that people like the Schuster family were the Sloven Gypsy kind, Bohemians, therefore he had to hit him. A confused Sepp still did not understand. He had no idea what Gypsy meant. Bohemian was another word he had not heard before. Was it all because they were not even Lutherans, like everybody else in the village? Sepp, just like his parents, was Catholic!

When anyone came to their home, Waldemar and Erika always invited them in, offered whatever they had to offer, some fruit, food or something to drink. Sepp's parents were doing their best to welcome visitors. A few times when Sepp went along with Erika to the one or the other farmer's home, they were asked to wait outside, never invited in, except the one time when it rained cats and dogs. Yes, Erika was asked to come out of the rain indoors, yet she was told to make sure to watch her boy so that he wouldn't touch anything. And they were not offered a chair to sit down but had to wait in the doorway. Uneasy about the treatment Sepp mentioned it to his sister Frieda, who told him: "Some people are afraid that if they let us in their homes, we take their things without asking!"

At the time a perplexed Sepp didn’t understand that refugees from the Sudetenland didn't count as much! They were just tolerated. Nevertheless, because of the much-needed services Waldemar rendered, they were accepted, somewhat, somehow. Yes, to gain the villager’s trust took a lot of time!

One-time boys chased a large pregnant sow through the fields, and it was Sepp who was accused of having caused her to lose her piglets. Sepp’s mother, even after Sepp said he didn’t do it, Erika decided to work for the farmer during harvest to make up for the loss of the piglets.

As kids, the children did play doctor, and impulsive Sepp wanted just to be a kid among kids! He didn't know some kids wanted to figure out what was different between them and him! If someone was willing to play with him, Sepp played.

Those other kids had relatives, had grandparents and friends; he had none of them. More often than not, a disappointed Sepp was alone among the children in Kleinerort. He had to get used to it, to being a loner. However, whenever he got away from the village and was exploring by himself the hills and wooded areas of the Steigerwald, he never felt alone. There was so much to see and so much to do.

It took some time, and then slowly Sepp understood. It wasn't that the other boys in the village of 24 homes wouldn't have played with him. It was that the parents of those kids were not letting them. At the time Sepp was still not able to figure out how his family got the house number 28.

One evening, a farmer Erika had helped harvesting potatoes, was bringing her a box with baby chickens, and he talked quite insensitive as a matter of fact about someone who had lost a lot of blood. He also explained in great detail how the woman who had been helping harvesting wheat, fell into a straw-baler. The story ended with the woman bleeding to death. Much appalled by what he heard Sepp fainted. Erika's conclusion was: "My son must be allergic to bloody stories!" And Erika put Sepp to bed with a sugar cube drenched with Klosterfrau Melissengeist, a German miracle elixir with 79% alcohol content. Ever since, whenever he felt sick, Sepp asked his mother for some of the miracle Melissengeist. Erika didn't know that Sepp had not fainted as a result of the talk about blood, he had fainted because he was visualizing the process how that woman went through a hay-baler and came out baled as a tightly bound square package.

Yes, Sepp's mother she always had an answer, she knew so many remedies whenever Sepp got sick. Looking back they had no access to a pharmacy, and the next doctor was about 10 kilometers away. He was working out of his home. However, most of the time the doctor was on the road on his motorcycle making house calls. One cold winter morning when Sepp touched the white metal of the wood-stove's pipe, the skin from his right hand got stuck there. Sepp's mother put egg-white onto his skinless hand immediately. Then she packed his hand with quark and bandaged it, it took some time, but healed very nicely.

By age four Sepp had wheels, his first bicycle. It was painted red. And it had three gears. The seat was damaged. Therefore, his father made a new seat for him, a small leather saddle. The bike was no kiddy bike. It was a medium size man's bike. It was fast. Young Sepp loved his bicycle. He was going places now. The roads were not the best, yet there was little traffic as very few people had a car. The local farmers used horse and wagon. And there was only one wood fired tractor in the village. Sepp remembered running a motorcycle off the road. When his father found out, he apologized and promised to make up for any damages.

Young Sepp had his accidents too. At age 5, he tumbled, head over, falling off his bike into a hornets' nest, all because he had his feet on the handlebars, and was going down the road too fast! According to his mother, he was comatose for six days. Sepp never found out if it was because of the fall or was it due to those hornet's stings? What he remembered was that after he had fallen, he was scared. A cloud of giant wasps was swarming around him. All he remembered was that he saw a woman's face, looking just like his mother, but older and she told him: "Get back on your bike now! You must come home!" He got on his bike chased by those hornets. He was pedaling fast and faster, trying to outrun their stingers, racing homeward, knowing he had to go home, get to his mother. He didn't remember how often he had been stung, neither that paralyzed he fell off his bike right in front of his mother, at their 'Häusle.'

At age five Sepp attended school for the first time. In Kleinerort all kids from 1st to 8th school-year were in one and the same classroom. Herr Hauptlehrer Meyer was their teacher. The 5 to 10-year-young were sitting up front, the 11 to 15-year-old in the back. Not too many younger German men were around these days, because of the war. Understandable then that Sepp had a teacher who was rather old. The first thing he taught Sepp was to write. He taught him how to write in 'Old German,' yes the old-fashioned way, Suetterlin style. Sepp had learned from his father how to write the alphabet, but that was a different writing, not what Hauptlehrer Meyer was asking him to do.

Herr Hauptlehrer Meyer was a good man! Sepp also got it with a ruler or a 'Rute!' Whenever that happened, he knew he had it coming because he had done something wrong. Herr Hauptlehrer Meyer was strict. All writing was done on black slate writing tablets. The front was lined, and the back had squares. The first year Sepp didn't get to use paper to write on, neither in class nor at home for the homework.

An iPad or just any tablet would have been nice to have; yet those didn't exist in 1955, not even in the most advanced dreams.

Determined to get all his homework done, Sepp had to do so as long as there was daylight. The 'Häusle' had no electricity. There were no power poles between the village and the dump. All homes in the community had power, and the schoolhouse had electricity too. Sepp's father used a petroleum lamp in his shop. A second oil lamp was carried from one room to the other, wherever light was needed.

In the kitchen, one wood stove with a large oven heated the entire house. In the back of the stove was an insert for water. Here they had 'brewed coffee' going all the time. What they called coffee was 'Kaffee Ersatz,' and no coffee bean had ever come near it. Waldemar had a small woodstove in his shop. They kept warm, even in the coldest of the winters.

Newspapers were never thrown away. After reading the news, it was used to wrap food. Once used, the paper was saved to light the fire in the stove. The newspaper also was utilized in the outhouse. Small square pieces held up by a nail were the luxury of toilette paper.

They also had running water in the form of a little creek, just outside. At the 'Häusle' they got water from a well. One always had to prime the pump, then hand-pump, pump, pump, pump, pump-pump, and pump. Their well's water was clean, rich in minerals.

Sepp's mother washed all the clothes in the little creek across the dirt road, at a spot where his father had installed a wooden board to dam enough water to fill several buckets at once. The brook's water was also used to water the garden, one bucket at a time.

From the 'Häusle' up the road past the dump, through the forest and over the hill just below the old castle, the dirt and gravel road led to a big valley with a farm known as Neuhof. The land in the valley belonged to an old noble family, still living in their modernized castle above vineyards atop a hill, about 5km past Hinterberg, from Neuhof it would have been about 10km. On his bike, Sepp, nosy as he was, surveyed the dirt roads in the valley around Neuhof. The gates at the Neuhof farm were closed, and it looked like no one was living at the place. Sepp stayed away from the fenced-in grounds.

Encouraged by the good farm roads, he kept on riding his bike. At an open grassy pasture with lots and lots of cherry trees, he stopped, parked his bike resting it against a tree and did some investigating. It was the cherry season, just seeing those bright red ripe fruits made him feeling hungry, and he viewed those tempting sweet delights dangling from the twigs. After stepping on those already fallen to the ground, he picked one up. In his hand, he held a nice looking, firm feeling, and delicious tasting red cherry. He compared it with a couple of cherries straight from the tree. Those were as good and practically grew right into his mouth. Sepp filled up on cherries and only after spitting a hundred or more cherry pits onto the ground, did he get back on his bike. He kept on riding around the paths on the Neuhof farm for another hour or two and visited an apple orchard and acres planted with plum trees. He looked at them too and was making sure he remembered where they are. For now, the plums were all still tiny and green. Sepp planned to return at harvest time.

Filled up with sweet fruits, getting thirsty, Sepp was finding his way back out of the valley on service roads between potato and wheat fields. Then once he reached the road below the castle, he saw their 'Häusle' in the distance. Energetic as fast as he could, Sepp was racing his bike down the hill towards home. Sepp noticed a deep and wide pothole in his way. But it was already too late, both brakes locked, sliding sideways slowed his fall. Sepp hit the ground head-on. He split his forehead wide open. All Sepp remembered was that he got up, looked at his bike, it was okay, but all he saw was a bloody red film. Sepp clearly saw in his mind a face just like his mother's face, but older, and heard her voice telling him: "You must come home now!" And doing as told, the injured Sepp got on his bike, seeing little of the road through a bloody red film, and he rode back home. His mother fainted when he arrived with an exposed skull and frontal bone and all covered in blood. She ran into the village, used the village's one and only telephone at the mayor's home, to call a taxi service in the next town, to take Sepp to a doctor. The doctor used iodine and needle and cotton and closed the open wound. At home, his mother gave him sugar cubes with Klosterfrau Melissengeist while Sepp told his mother about the face and the voice, and all she said was: "It's your Guardian Angel! Thank God, she watches over you!"

When young Sepp was in his second school year, Waldemar's son, Karl Schuster sent his father as a birthday present a hand-crank-operated Siemens shortwave radio. Waldemar was listening to the radio on and off.

What happened in the late fall of 1956 was that the radio news reported Russian troops had overrun Hungary. Sepp didn't know enough about the relationship between Sudetenland and Hungary. Therefore he did not fully comprehend the meaning of the 'Hungarian capital has fallen.' But Sepp understood the expression on his parents' faces. He noticed that both Erika and Waldemar were acting panicky, being scared and afraid of a Russian invasion. A worried Erika asked: "Where can we go? What if the Russians decide to invade us here too?" and Waldemar answered in an alarmed tone: "Why would the Americans defend us against the Russians. Or the Brits, or the Frogs?"

"You think they have no interest in protecting us?" She wondered. Waldemar pointed out: "They didn't do so, as promised to those left in Hungary, why would they care about us Germans?" And Erika with tears: "All we had, all is put in the 'Häusle' we have no money to go anyplace!" "Oh ja! Maybe we should have thought of it before. South America was good to Karl, too late now!" Waldemar surrendered to the facts. Waldemar didn't argue with Erika who was saying: "Nothing in God's world happens without reason. We just don't know what his will is for us!" And as they didn't have the means to leave, they stayed, and both prayed. That was the only time Sepp saw and heard his father say a prayer.

In the years to follow, Sepp found out more about how the Germans were treated by the Russian occupying forces in East Germany. By then he understood why his parents didn't want to be in the Russian Zone.

Waldemar used his bicycle around the village and to deliver shoes to the farmers in the village, as well as for his daily trip to a farmer to get his 1-liter-milk-can refilled with milk fresh from the cows. For rides to Unterschwarzenberg Waldemar used his Zuendapp Moped. A fellow he had met in Unterschwarzenberg sold Waldemar a used Adler motorcycle. A happy Waldemar brought it home and took it apart and put it back together. He made sure all was cleaned, greased and oiled and in good running condition. As he was doing so, Sepp eager for knowledge, inquisitive watched his father assembling the Adler motorcycle. Waldemar handed Sepp some tools and encouraged him to take his bicycle apart too. Piece by piece they disassembled the bike and Waldemar helped Sepp to put it all back together. He was making sure that Sepp knew what and where to grease and oil and when to tighten and how tight the chain needed to be, to have his bike in top shape.

The same week, Sepp had an opportunity to assist his father and to help Waldemar as he fixed a flat tire on his bicycle. The day after fixing Waldemar's flat tire, Sepp had a flat too, and his father told him to fix it, and Sepp did it. He was quite proud of doing it all by himself. The same day Waldemar added a leather tool bag to Sepp's bike. In the same were: rubber patches, cut from an old tube, a small piece of sandpaper, rubber glue and the tools needed to remove a tire as well as a 16 in 1 bicycle wrench. His father also gave him a 'next to new' bicycle pump. As Sepp was adjusting the tension for the chain on his bike, one of the local farmers was dropping off a pair of boots in need of repair. Waldemar asked him if he had another old pair of boots, because the leather on these was so old and worn, that it needed to be replaced. The man said: “I bring it later to you!” Sepp listened to them talk about the number of women in Kleinerort and elsewhere. Sepp overheard his father saying: “That may change because American soldiers like to take German women home with them as war souvenirs from the Reich!” “Jawohl, that's to show off to their neighbors in America, by bringing a living trophy from the big war they had fought and won!” the visitor claimed.

Next day at school, Siegfried, a boy Sepp's age became a hero to the village girls. During breaks and in the schoolyard, Siegfried had to show them his little wiener. He had fallen into barbed wire and survived it. There was not much to see. Siegfried had a tiny penis, shrunk and wrinkled. Three stitches had mended the rip in the foreskin. He showed his wound if asked. It was healing fast. Sepp watched him dropping his pants as two girls had a closer look. One was lifting his little manhood, and the other was playing with his balls. She remarked: “I see, but look, our goat has much bigger balls than you!”

The other mentioned: “You should see the ‘Schwanz’ of our horse. It is as long as my arm!” Both girls were laughing, and Siegfried looked happy, because of the attention he got.

All the American soldiers were everywhere well liked and most welcome in Kleinerort. Everyone loved those gifts of cigarettes, chewing gums, canned food, and chocolates as handed out by the American soldiers. The locals called them lovingly Amis (Aaammeees) because they loved the guys. The Care-packages, food from America, also helped, and were highly appreciated.

Over in Kitzingen where many of the American soldiers were stationed, the word was out that single women stayed in line to get themselves an Ami boyfriend. From what was said, the soldiers preferred only the young and cute ones. Sepp was also told that black enlisted men, often were not able to date blond women at home; that's what they were looking for here in Bavaria. And it was no secret that German Fräulein from brunette to blonde, blue-eyed to hazelnut, skinny to the full-figured ones, all looked forward to meeting an American soldier. The daughter of the owner of the local brewery and Gasthaus Zum Lamm was pregnant and talking about going with her American boyfriend, soon to be husband, back to Alabama in America. She, 20 years old, had everyone jealous. She kept on saying: "Everybody in America owns a new home, with bathrooms and shower, and all kitchens have a refrigerator, they also have radio and movies out of a box, called TV. Everybody has a telephone and a garage with a nice big car or even two, and all the food anyone can dream of!" Everyone in Kleinerort had food, nobody had a car, and nobody had a refrigerator. Every third home had a working radio, and as for television those Amis talked about, 'movies out of a box,' nobody in Kleinerort had seen a TV yet. Rumor was that they had TV in the major cities, with a single channel, available only at certain times of the day. By now the villagers were proud of having four telephones. There was one at each Gasthaus, one at the grocery store, and the other at the Mayor's home.

Well, yeah and behind the Gasthaus Zum Lamm, Sepp attempted to climb over an old tall wooden fence, he got to the top, then the wooden structure fell on him. He was incapable of lifting it up. It was too heavy for him. It buried Sepp! And being there trapped, the weighty fence squeezed the air out of his chest. While being pressed into the ground, Sepp did see the woman's face, looking much like his mother but older, and heard the woman's voice telling him: "You can't do that to me. I need you to go home now." Lucky for him two strong men saw Sepp's struggle under the fence and raised it up, and the boy could get out from underneath. Half numb, Sepp stumbled as fast as he could across freshly plowed fields home.

A well-dressed businessman from Nuremberg stopped by Waldemar's shoe-repair-shop. He arrived by car and needed one shoe repaired because the heel had broken off. Waldemar asked him to wait. He offered him a glass of Franken-wine. Sepp's father commented on the excellent quality of the man's shoes.

As the visitor waited, he talked about the farmers near Nuremberg who now had anything you could think off. According to him, they had silver candle holders, silver cutlery, jewelry, carpets, whatever, all due to the city dwellers who had been trading valuables with farmers, to get some food on the table. While reattaching the heel, Waldemar mentioned to him: "Here, the farmers are not wealthy, they just get by!" "Yes, they are too far away from any bombed out bigger city." The visitor replied. “Not just recently, all the past years when there has been no money! No! Many people still barter, money is scarce!” Waldemar stated. And he knew it, because most of the shoe repairs he did, were paid for in trade. The visitor did offer to pay Waldemar with rationing coupons, yet Sepp’s father looked at them and handed them back. He had no use for those because: “We get our milk, butter, bread, and our beer from the locals, all in trade, they don’t take coupons! Danke! No!” And the visitor paid with newly minted Deutsche Marks instead.

Almost all the homes in Kleinerort were built generations ago from sandstone, from local sandstone quarries, solid, meter thick walls. Luckily no bombs had leveled any of them. The church up on the hill, sitting in the middle of the graveyard, was a newer building, much more modern than some of those old homes in the village. It was the Lutheran church. Kleinerort was Lutheran, as the church so were all the people in Sepp's village. Lutheranism had spread to Kleinerort around 1700, before then it was Catholic since the days of 'Karl der Grosse' also known as Charlemagne.

Sepp's parents were Catholics, and when it came to God, Sepp learned fast that there was a difference. He soon started to think that there were two Gods, the Lutheran one who was kind to the people in his village, and a Catholic God who lived somewhere else. The nearest Catholic Church was in Hinterberg. If Sepp wanted to talk to his God, he had to go to Hinterberg. That was a long walk, about 3 km, over the hill. Waldemar had told him: "There are several different kinds of beliefs, and every side thinks their 'way of thinking' is better. But listen, my boy, there is only one God! Different people just have different names for him!"

Quite fascinated by the church's history and the Bible stories, young Sepp did his duties as an Altar boy in the Catholic Church, in Hinterberg, the little village over the hill. As he lived in an 'Evangelischen,' a Lutheran community, yet his family being 'Katholisch,' he had to travel the short distance of 3 kilometers to church services, sometimes on foot, most of the time on his bicycle. Sepp's father never went to church.

Young Sepp spent a lot of time alone in the forests in the hills surrounding Kleinerort. Often he dragged a fallen tree branch back home, as he knew that they always needed firewood. Waldemar seeing Sepp coming with some wood got his hatchet out and chopped it all into stove size pieces. Sepp liked the forest, but he always made sure he found his way back home. Yes, Sepp was an active child, lots of fresh air, an explorer and adventurer, an outsider too! Was he supposed to be a loner?

Sepp's father worked as long as there was daylight, and longer sometimes using his petroleum lamp. He did not have much time for Sepp. His mother worked in the fields at times from sunrise to past sunset. Yes, she too had not much time to attend to him. He kept busy, either on his bicycle or on foot, Sepp explored the surrounding hills and the many vestiges from the dark ages. He enjoyed visiting the ruins, remains of castles and fortresses where robber barons once lived. There was no lack of stone towers and walls of fortifications from medieval times. Virtually every hill had remnants from a bygone era and a robber baron story to go with it.

A bicycle arrived, an 18-gear bike, 3-gear spokes up front, six in the back. Waldemar's daughter, Traude had sent it from Berlin. It was pulchritudinous, and it came partially assembled. An overjoyed Sepp under the watchful eyes of his father put it all together. It was blue. Sepp liked red better. However, it was a special edition, and therefore he didn't care about the color much longer than maybe a minute. Sepp greased the chain and adjusted the tension just right. He tested the latest model of a snap-on-dynamo. Pushing a lever the little generator via a rubber wheel was getting its power from the front tire and thus then powered the headlamp and the tail-light. The brakes as well were so much better than what he had before. The new bike had side pull brakes with extra-long rubber inserts. He had barely broken his bike in, that Sepp had another fall and split his chin open. Such added a new scar, after nine stitches! But that time, at his latest accident he didn't see a face or heard a voice. Somehow he thought because he had not gone to Church for the past two Sundays, his 'Guardian Angel' had abandoned him.

With his chin still hurting, Sepp went for a week or longer every day down to the river. He had spotted a Hecht, a fish belonging to the Esox Lucius fish group, and known for feeding on other fish and frogs. Good firm meet, hard to get. No! Sepp didn't have fishing or hunting rights. He just had an idea that it may be an excellent addition to the dinner table. The next visit to see the Hecht, Sepp brought his bow, and one arrow tipped with a 5-centimeter long on both sides sharpened knife blade. Sepp sat down and as he had done on several days before, quiet and motionless he watched the Hecht in its spot next to the reeds, close to the embankment. Then Sepp positioned his bow and arrow. He aimed straight down on the Hecht's head. With his fingers on the bowstring, he built up the tension, and let go. There was movement. The water turned dirty gray. The arrow stuck firmly embedded in the mud and clay soil. Sepp watched the Hecht swimming up stream. After retrieving his arrow, disappointed but not ready to give up, Sepp waited for the water to clear. He imagined the tastiness of the fish, the mild, subtle flavor, firm, sweet white meat, and medium flakes. The Hecht was big enough to feed four. Intrigued by the challenge Sepp went home. Here, in the little creek at the 'Häusle,' he practiced and perfected for several days his aim to hit a submerged object located 20 to 30 centimeter deep in the water. Satisfied with his newly acquired 'bow and arrow underwater hunting skills' he went back to see if the Hecht was still there and it was. Next day armed with bow and arrow Sepp attempted the second kill. Using as much tension as possible, Sepp shot the knife tipped arrow with all his might. That time it nailed the Hecht through the head. But Sepp wasn't done yet. He worked hard to drag and carry the big fish from the water to his bike, and to get it into an empty potato sack. Finally, he shouldered the bag and got on his bicycle. One hand held the bag, as he was driving with his free hand. The bagged wiggling fish rested against his lower back and on the luggage rack of the bike as Sepp pedaled home.

His father was very pleased about the catch, and he filleted the fish, after cleaning the bite in Sepp's hand and adding iodine and a bandage. Yes, the Hecht had bitten Sepp's hand when he first attempted to take the fish out of the bag.

The same month Herr Hauptlehrer Meyer was talking about his friend Dr. Sauer who had the fishing and hunting rights near Kleinerort. "Professor Sauer has been observing a Hecht, part of the Esox Lucius fish group for the past year. It is a first rate example of a Hecht, and it is known to feed on frogs and fish in the river south of Kleinerort. It made its home near the old wooden bridge. My friend Dr. Sauer has shared with me the Hecht's location, for a school project. It is worth seeing, so kids let's go for a walk. Go down there and see if we can spot the Hecht!" They made several trips to see the Hecht on different days but never got to see the Hecht; the one Hauptlehrer Meyer had promised them.

Erika was pleased. That year they had fresh fish twice. During the year the Schuster family didn't see much fish on the table. Once or twice a year, they had a salted herring and steamed potatoes. It changed just before the cold weather added a layer of ice to lakes and rivers. In late October the local fish-pond was emptied, and Franconia carp (fish) became available to everyone in the village. The first year they had carp, Erika filleted the fish, and fried the filets. After talking with several of the local farmers' wives who had been preparing carp every year, Erika added new recipes to her 'cookbook.' One year she cooked the carp 'blue' stewed in a broth made from beer and vinegar. The next time she split the carp in the middle lengthwise and battered and baked the fish. Waldemar liked the baked carp best. Sepp thought the carp 'blue' in beer soup was much better.

At age 7 Sepp had his First Communion in Hinterberg, in a church much older than the Lutheran church in Kleinerort. Hinterberg's church was original built in 1414 but only completed, 200 years later. That Catholic Church combined features of Gothic, Renaissance, and early Baroque styles. Tilman Riemenschneider, one of the greatest German sculptors of the 15th century, had carved many of the church figurines from wood. At the First Communion Sepp received the Sacrament of the Holy

Eucharist, which is the eating of consecrated bread and drinking of consecrated wine. Erika asked him the question: “How did it feel?” Sepp wasn’t sure, but people were kneeling down every Sunday for the pastor to get one of those empty tasting round cakes, and about the wine, he didn’t know enough about wine to judge the same. “Ja! It is what I have to do, being Catholic!” He said, and his mother nodded her head.

At the beginning of winter, Traude Schuster, Waldemar’s daughter and Sepp’s stepsister in Berlin, sent him a sled, a metal racing sled. Sepp had never met her, but he liked Traude a lot. She had sent him books, a flashlight, a pocketknife, an excellent set of ice-skates, roller-skates, and his most cherished possession the 18-gear racing bike. All he knew about her was that she was Waldemar’s daughter from his previous marriage and that she was a nurse, who worked and lived in Berlin, and that she was just a few years younger than Erika, his mother. His father had told him a little more after Sepp returned from his first few test-drives with the new sled. He said: “Traude is an unusual woman! She is much like her mother was. She likes to help. She cares. And she wants to make people happy.” Then Waldemar added: “Traude always wanted to be a nurse, and when she started at the Charité all her dreams came true. She wanted to work in a hospital. She wanted to learn from the best and work with the most famous doctors, yes she collaborated with Dr. Sauerbruch a highly recognized surgeon, he had written books, he was in a film, and he was instrumental in the development of many breakthroughs in medicine. Already as a young man in Breslau, he became famous for developing the Sauerbruch chamber. He was one of the greatest, and Traude would have done so well if there wouldn’t have been the ‘verdammte Krieg’ (damned war)!” Sepp who had heard the phrase ‘damned war’ before, was heading back out and enjoyed the snow.

In the snow and on the ice, Sepp was real hell with his metal sled. No hill was safe from him, the indestructible ‘Fluechtlings Junge.’ Sepp wasn’t easily scared. Told that he couldn't because nobody could, he rode his sled over a ski-ramp, several times, flying quite a distance through the air. Every time luckily he landed, on top of his sled with all the air knocked out of him. Sepp showed those who had doubts that he could do it. He didn't realize that he could easily have killed himself, and if the sled would have been a wooden one, it may have broken apart on impact, while landing during the first jump.

One morning when school was out, Sepp rode his sled down a narrow forest road between pine trees. The sled picked up an excellent speed on the icy ground, then after hitting a rock, he drifted off the path and collided with a tree. After the initial impact, Sepp felt nothing. Paralyzed unable to move, not feeling his fingers or his feet, he spent hours under the trees in and half-buried under the snow. All day he could not move. At some point, his mind was busy thinking: "Ja! Is this now what it feels to be dead? What about heaven or hell? Don't just forget about me here. I want to go someplace! Where am I?"

Then as darkness arrived, Sepp felt like someone was urging him to get up. He heard the voice telling him: "You must get up now!" And he saw a face like his mother's face but older. Then he noticed he could move his legs, and his arms. Soon after, Sepp was able to get up, and he was not leaving without his beloved sled, so he dragged the same and himself home. In the cold snow, his body should have been frozen stiff. What powers allowed him to get up? And Sepp did talk with his mother about the voice and face, and she put her arms around him and said: "I know! My son has a Guardian Spirit, a personal angel, thank God for her!"

Sepp's mother, he called her Ma, or Erika, insisted that he went during school vacation time to winter or summer camp whenever possible. She may not have had the time to spend all days mothering him, but she was always there when he needed her. Once she had heard about the availability of summer and winter camps provided for school-kids by various organizations, Erika found a way to get Sepp signed up.

Shortly after his sled adventure, he was in a winter camp, in Hof near the Eastern border, the iron curtain. Aside from learning and playing, the kids also got a proper physical check up at the youth camp. Sepp ended up with a special gypsum cast, in which he had to lie while sleeping. He also had to do stretch exercises on a regular basis during the day. That youth camp had turned into a real bummer. Sepp was treated like he had some back issues, which he had not, or had he? Returning home, with the gypsum cast, Erika made certain that he slept in the cast till he outgrew the same which was within the year.

Either one of the various 'accidents' could have finished young Sepp's life, but did not. Why did he survive? What spared him? All Sepp could think off was what he had heard before in Church, namely that there are angels, and that they can and may look out for you. His mother had said: "It's your Guardian Angel!" But then why didn't the woman he saw have wings? The angels he had seen in paintings and those carved and displayed at church, they all had a pair of wings!

While tirelessly working in the fields, Erika always made sure they all had a good meal.

Erika helped the local farmers doing fieldwork. They in return provided food they otherwise didn't have. Erika didn't get paid much for her hard work! Money was scarce. The usual pay was in goods, chickens, rabbits, butter, and the right to second harvest from the harvested fields. For the past three years, Erika's pay from the Schaefer family included a one-year-old pig, slaughtered at the onset of winter. That year Erika walked her pig back home from the Schaefer farm, where it was raised. They kept it in a small pigpen, until Herr Schlachter, an experienced slaughter, and local meat inspector arrived. Herr Schlachter shot the pig with a stun gun in the head. Then Waldemar and Herr Schlachter strung the pig up by the hind legs, the back down and belly up onto a sturdy wooden ladder. Then they lifted it up on one end. Everyone helped, Erika, Sepp, and the two men righted the ladder against the barn's wall. Head down, the pig was hanging from the top of the ladder leaning against the building, and Herr Schlachter bled it. Erika was busy catching the blood in a large bowl for later use in blood sausage. After the flow of blood had stopped, Herr Schlachter cut the pig open, and piece-by-piece removed all the internal organs. Waldemar emptied and washed and cleaned the stomach and the intestines. Those were all needed and reused as casings to be stuffed later during the sausage making process. After gutting the carcass Herr Schlachter cut the head off first, then the front legs and the rest of the body was split before being portioned. Herr Schlachter cut the pig into sections for roast, chops, hams, ribs, bacon, Speck and Schinken. Not much got wasted. All meat was being used. All large and small pieces of fat were collected and cooked on the stove in a large pot to extract the lard to be used throughout the year for cooking, baking, and frying. Here Herr Schlachter, with a handshake and picking up the two pairs of shoes Waldemar had repaired for him, left to take care of another job still waiting for him on the same day.

Waldemar and Erika salted most of the meat and stored it. Next day Erika rubbed all the meat to be smoked several times with garlic before being hung in the smoke-room above the kitchen stove. Having a wood fire going all winter long not only cured the meat in the smoke-box, but it also provided the meat with a distinct smoke-flavor. Sepp did ask: "Ja! Why don't we slaughter a pig in the summer? On a warmer day, instead of when it's freezing!" Waldemar explained: "You do best when it's cold, because of the maggots and flies, and the meat going bad unless you have a way to chill or cook it!" Then Waldemar pointed out: "Listen, when I was young we had to skin the pig before cutting it up, and we used the pigskin to make leather for jackets and gloves."

Erika was busy for several days with cutting and grinding up the innards and meat trimmings for sausages. Sepp helped, by doing as told by his mother. For the sausages, Erika was grinding up herbs, garlic, and the salted and peppered chopped meat and organ pieces. Sepp watched Waldemar firmly holding the casings onto the funnel at the end of the meat grinder as Erika was turning the handle. Slowly the meat passed the 'Meat Grinder and Sausage Stuffer' and filled the shells. Every about 15-centimeter Waldemar tied a string to show the end and beginning of a serving of sausage. Sepp's task was to add the sausages to a large pot. Here those sausages were cooked first, before being cured in the smoke chamber. All in all, the yearly meat preparation and the sausage-making project took the better part of a week to finish. That was also the only week that they had meat every day. Usually, they had meat once, very seldom twice a week.

Sepp's mother also raised chickens, rabbits, and goats. And they had a dog and two cats. Those outdoor cats lived on rodents, and once in a while, a bird as well. Those cats earned their keep and were rewarded by getting fresh milk every day. On the small plot of land, Erika had planted berry bushes, apple trees, potatoes, rhubarb, cabbage, garlic, and a variety of seasonal vegetable. They did not starve. Sepp always had plenty to eat.

Sepp had proper shoes too. His father took care of him. As winter had arrived, Sepp needed gloves, warm gloves. One of their cats had gone missing; the gloves were warm and lined with fur, same color, and the same type of the cat he never saw again.

Since his fifth year, Sepp had been going to the Volksschule (primary school) in Kleinerort. His teacher, Herr Hauptlehrer Meyer was strict.

Sepp remembered the wooden stick he used, to beat the hand of any of the kids in class, those who didn't provide full attention. If the homework wasn't done, as it should have been, the punishment was a beating on the butt. It was the teacher's choice, pants up or pants down. Sepp's leather pants got beaten a few times, but they could handle it. During Sepp's first four years in school, he was sitting up front. His sister was in her last four years of school, therefore sat in the very back row. She got to watch Sepp getting it with a ruler, with a willow reed, and one-time Hauptlehrer Meyer even gave her brother a good spanking using his bare hand, on his butt, in front of the class. When Frieda said to Sepp: "I cried watching Herr Meyer..." and "...it must have hurt!" he answered her: "Ja! A little, not much, my lederhosen have two layers of leather. They are strong!"

His sister, Frieda, always helped her mother after school. Reaching age 14, it was time for her to learn a trade. Frieda was accepted for an apprenticeship in Neustadt, a city a few hours away. Frieda's employment came with live-in quarters while she learned to make flags and do embroidery. Around the time that Frieda got ready to leave for Neustadt, to start her apprenticeship, our Sepp got another beating in school. Someone had removed all the chalk from the basket at the chalkboard. Then Herr Meyer had to stop because the ruler broke. Or maybe he stopped because he believed Sepp, who over and over had assured Herr Hauptlehrer that he would never do such a thing, because it's stealing, and he did not take the chalk sticks. Somewhat irritated Sepp talked with his sister about the chalk incident. That's when Frieda confessed, and she asked him not to tell mother. Frieda too had been disciplined by Herr Hauptlehrer Meyer. "And I didn't do anything wrong at school!" she added. Frieda explained: "Two times, and not in front of the class, but in the storage room next door." According to Frieda, Herr Meyer screamed angrily and shouted: "Stop giving my boys the wrong ideas. We don't like your kind tempting them!" Frieda told Sepp that Hauptlehrer Mayer had her over the old desk, the dress up, panties down. And spitting in his hands, Herr Hauptlehrer Mayer had spanked her till she cried. Hearing how his sister had been mistreated made Sepp real angry.

Frieda added: “Think I am lying? I am not!”

Sepp was fuming. It was on the same afternoon that he went back to the schoolhouse and let himself in through the window. He knew where the chalk was kept, and he took all the chalk supplies and dropped them in the outhouse. Sepp felt better, and to himself, he said "Ja! I was already punished, for stealing chalk, so what?" The next day in school, Sepp’s expectations were disappointed. Herr Hauptlehrer Meyer didn’t say a word when he couldn’t find any chalk to write on the board. He went back to his apartment above the schoolhouse and returned just a few minutes later with a handful of chalk.

Looking back, Sepp knew that Herr Hauptlehrer Meyer had seen something in him. Maybe he just wanted to get Sepp out of his classroom, because somehow he, Sepp, didn’t fit in with the village kids in Kleinerort? Once Sepp had learned to read, he read everything he could find. There were many words he did not fully understand, but he kept on reading. Herr Hauptlehrer Meyer gave Sepp highest marks, and he did suggest to his mother that Sepp needed to leave, after just four years of

Volksschule. According to Hauptlehrer Meyer, his school did not offer enough for a talented youngster like Sepp. He talked Erika Schuster into getting Sepp some higher, better education and sending him to the Oberrealschule (High School) in another town, in Unterschwarzenberg.

Yes, Herr Hauptlehrer Meyer did his part to get Sepp out of there. Did he know that his actions assured Sepp would go and see the world away from Kleinerort?

After Sepp's sister, Frieda, had left to start her apprenticeship in Neustadt, several boys her age and older from Kleinerort, asked Sepp about her. What a surprise for Sepp, as he had no idea that she had made so many friends in the village, while he had only one. That one was Siegfried. It was also Siegfried who told Sepp about Frieda: "When your mother was working for us in the fields, your sister Frieda used to watch the older boys play soccer. She played sometimes. Your sister does know how to kick a ball. My older brother talked about skinny-dipping in the fish-pond with your sister." Sepp recalled Frieda's telling him about getting a beating from an angry Hauptlehrer Meyer, and he asked himself: "Did Frieda's hanging out with the village boys have something to do with Herr Meyer getting mad, angry enough, that he slapped her naked butt real hard at the schoolhouse?"

A week later Siegfried's older brother and two other older boys cornered Sepp outside the schoolhouse and wanted to know "Where is your sister now?" "When will she be back?" "She is coming back isn't she?" They accused him of being a liar when he said: "I don't know!" Sepp found Siegfried and asked him: "Your brother and his friends called me a liar, they want to see my sister. Why? What's going on?" And this time Siegfried told him all he knew. He elucidated: "Your sister was hanging out with several of the older boys. My brother and his friends said she was well developed for her age, not boring like the village girls. Your Frieda was the one who showed them 'French Letters' and explained to them how to use protection. No, Frieda Bauer was not shy at all. She also knew everything about 'French Kissing' too!" And Sepp didn't know what 'French Letters' were or what 'French Kissing' meant, all he knew was that his father and others called the French 'frogs!' Yes he knew about the princess who kissed a frog, and the frog became a prince, somehow it all must be connected, so he thought.

Once Frieda started her apprenticeship, she only came home twice within the year. Therefore Sepp did not see much of his sister. One day when Frieda was visiting; Sepp overheard her telling her mother: "I'm not Waldemar's daughter. I don't even have his name. I am Frieda Bauer. I don't feel at home here!" After Frieda had finished her apprenticeship in Neustadt, she was busy dating and living with various men, in different towns, but none were from Kleinerort. As only very few people had a telephone, and Sepp's parents did not, the only news they got from Frieda, was whenever she visited. Being busy herself, that didn't happen too often.

To live in the American zone, near Kitzingen, had many advantages. Often enough Amis, as they called them, had their military exercises in the surrounding forests. Erika, who was worried about Frieda, because nobody had seen her for a few months, now was also concerned about Sepp, because he liked to visit the areas where the American soldiers had their training maneuvers. The Amis they had plenty of everything: Chewing gum, chocolate, cigarettes, canned food! They had it all, and they handed those treasures out like there was an unlimited supply. Everybody in Kleinerort knew the Amis as rich folks.

These days Sepp liked two village girls. One was Gunda the other was Christa. Both girls had been copying his homework for quite some time. They always came to him when they needed something. Gunda was short with long dark hair, and Christa was tall and blond. Being needed and wanted, made him feel special. No wonder, Sepp had the hots for them, yet they not for him. He knew why! He was Catholic. He was a 'Nobody!' It all changed during those times he had chewing gum and American chocolate to hand out. Then Christa, as well as Gunda, was swarming around him like flies. They left him standing where he was and ran off back home or wherever to, once he ran out of the much-desired treats.

What a surprise? When Sepp got to the schoolhouse, Sepp saw a new face. They had a new student at the school in Kleinerort, his name was Mel, and his real name as Sepp soon found out was Melchior named after one of the Holy Three Kings. Mel's parents had moved in at Neuhof as the new caretakers of the Neuhof farm. Mel's mother was from the Schwabenland. Her husband was from Romania. Mel's father was an African soldier. Mel was black, had short curly hair, and he was very friendly, yet many of the kids in the class ignored him. Sepp shared some of the food Erika had packed for him with Mel, because for some reason his mother hadn't provided any snacks for him to take to school. Later Sepp walked home with Mel as they were heading the same way, except Mel had another kilometer and a half to go. They got to talk and became friends on Mel's first day at school. Mel was smart, smarter than most kids his age. He had gone to school in Cologne, the big city on the Rhine River. That's where Melchior's grandparents lived. When Waldemar saw Mel, he called him a 'war baby,' whatever it meant. Sepp called him "My friend Mel." Mel invited Sepp to come by and visit and meet his mother and her husband. Sepp had only once been back to the Neuhof since his big accident, the one that gave him the scar on the forehead, several years ago. He was eager to visit Mel and the Neuhof farm. The first opportunity to see his friend Mel came on a Sunday. After coming back home from church in Hinterberg, Sepp rode up the hill on the road below the castle, into the Neuhof valley. The gate to the farm was now open. Mel greeted him and took him inside the kitchen of the main building. His mother's name was Ursula. She gave him a big hug: "Gruess Gott, little man! Thank you many times for sharing your food with my son." Next, she offered to feed both of them. Neither one was hungry. The boys had better plans. Mel wanted to show Sepp around. Sepp wanted to see what there was to see at Neuhof.

Mel first provided Sepp with a (Christian) history lesson: "See, the origin of my mother's name, Ursula is named after the Saint of Cologne. That's where she is from. The history about St. Ursula goes in many different directions. Some say she was the daughter of a King on her way to Rome; others say she was the leader of a group of virgins who refused to marry a Hun leader. It is also said she was the leader of a small group of women who got killed near Cologne. However, others say she was the leader of 11 thousand maidens and 60 thousand common women who got tortured near Cologne. Only God knows the truth. The fact is that at the beginning of the fourth century a Senator by the name of Clematius built a church to honor a group of women who had been martyred at Cologne. My grandparents pray to St. Ursula. It's their guardian saint."

"Ja! My mother said I have a Guardian Angel too!" Sepp said. Mel agreed: "See! My guardian is King Melchior!" Then Mel explained: "See, I was named Melchior not only because King Melchior's body was brought to Cologne by Barbarossa the Holy Roman Emperor, but also because I was born on Holy Three Kings Day (also known as Epiphany.) When I was born, so my grandmother said, as she saw me coming out she knew that I looked just like one of the Holy Three Kings, and when she asked my grandfather he suggested: 'That one looks like Melchior the dark one of the Three Kings, and that was it. Ever since, I am Melchior. Asking my mother about my father, all she knows is that he was an African soldier and spoke French, like so many men serving in the military after the war, at least in the French Zone, in Schwaben, where she worked and lived at the time. Ulrich, her husband, is taking care of us and is the only father I know, he married my mother when I was real little!"

"Ja! So you have a King as guardian, and birthday on Holy Three King's Day, a 'double whammy' you are twice protected!" Sepp remarked. "See, Sepp we are Catholics! There is no Catholic church in Kleinerort? Or is there?" Sepp answered with, "Ja! Not in Kleinerort! But in Hinterberg!" And they walked over to a grassy fenced area. In the pasture were four small horses. Mel explained: "See! Those are Bosnian Ponies; that's how big they get. My father imported them from Romania!"

"Ja! Can you ride them like real horses?" Sepp wanted to know. As if he had been waiting for the question Mel walked over to the ponies and started talking to them. Next, he climbed on one waving Sepp to join him: "See! Come on let's go for a ride, take Dumitro!" Mel pointed at the gray-brownish pony, "See, Dumitro is very friendly and multi-talented a good riding and pack horse." Sepp didn't need to be asked twice.

He climbed on Dumitro, and the pony followed Mel's Bosnian horse. Sepp had a lot of fun exploring the farm on horseback.

As they returned to the farmhouse, Mel told Sepp about his grandparents and the big city: "See, in Cologne, my grandparents live near the Rhine River. It's not far from the big stores, and I can walk to my big schoolhouse, with many classrooms, many teachers, and my grandma she can cook. She cooks food from all over the world! See, Cologne is not like Kleinerort with only one general store, in the city we have streets lined with stores." Sepp listened and dreamed about the world outside of Kleinerort. "Ja! You have seen so much already, and you know so much. I haven't seen anything but Kleinerort. When I grow up, I want to see it all. I am looking forward to doing some traveling myself." After that initial visit with Mel, Sepp went to the Neuhof farm a couple more times before getting ready for the Oberrealschule. The last time he got to ride Dumitro, he was so busy looking around, that's when he saw Mel taking off. Sepp urged Dumitro to follow by kicking him with his boots. Dumitro took off. He was galloping along but came to a sudden stop at the large wooden water trough in their path. With no saddle, riding bareback, nothing to hang onto, Sepp found himself splashing around in a 'kiddie-pool-size' water trough. Dumitro just stood there and stared at him motionless while watching a very embarrassed Sepp taking a full bath. Dumitro's big eyes had the 'I feel sorry' look. And maybe he did, but Sepp knew better Dumitro had been getting even for being kicked in the belly. Mel offered Sepp some dry clothing, but as it was a warm day, Sepp got on his bike and raced home. On the way, the wind was blow-drying his hair.

A few months before his 10th birthday, Sepp was enrolled in classes at the Oberrealschule (High-school) 18 kilometers from home, in Unterschwarzenberg. The Oberrealschule was a large new spacious three story building. The offices were on the ground floor. The rest were all classrooms. Quite amazed by the spaciousness Sepp counted twenty labs and classrooms. Religion, Latin, English, and French were on the lesson plan in addition to Mathematics, Geography, Biology, and Music. On a display board, it showed the number of currently enrolled students as 380, of which 310 were boys and only 70 girls. In Kleinerort the classroom attendance was a low of 18 and a high of 24, about 50/50 girls and boys. In front of the Oberrealschule was a large open area where the students could gather. Right next to it was the 'Fussballfeld' the soccer field. Sepp had never seen a soccer field that size with benches for visitors and grass as green as here. He had played soccer in the dirt behind the school in Kleinerort, on and off, during a break between classes. The large soccer field here looked so much more promising.

Each class had its classroom and its teacher. It was not like in Kleinerort, where Herr Hauptlehrer Meyer taught writing, languages, and history in the same room for all. In the first week at school, Sepp got to meet his teachers. A nun from the Franciscan order taught Latin. Two older professors lectured Geography and Biology. For Mathematics they had a young woman instructor. For English and French, both teachers were older women. An older gentleman, a pastor instilled the knowledge about religion. Religion was a must do class, each student had to attend. The same pastor was also in charge of the Catholic Boys Boarding House. That was an old 2-story building, once used as military barracks, just across the street. The Music classes were led by a couple, a husband and wife team. The music teachers were young in their late twenties. Here at the Oberrealschule, they used so many new words Sepp hadn't heard before from Herr Hauptlehrer Meyer.

From the first day on Sepp had been looking forward to playing soccer. It wasn't until the second week that Sepp got to kick a 'Fussball.' They had their sports class next to the soccer field in a big hall, a building mainly used for Handball. After some warm-up and exercises, the Physical Education teacher let all the boys show their talents in eleven-meter kicks. Sepp had fun with it and he joined the soccer team. Three weeks later once he had spent all Saturday afternoons and Sundays all day, in Unterschwarzenberg, not counting the other five days in school, he realized that it was something for the boys living in Unterschwarzenberg. It was asking too much from anyone having to commute and pedal 15 respectively 18 kilometers each way, on his bike to and from school. Erika told him: “Sepp seven days in school is too much!” She also was reminding him about homework and going to church on Sundays. Sepp had to admit his mother was right.

After about a month of getting settled in at school, Sepp finally found time to see his friend Mel again. Ursula greeted him, and that time he also met her husband Ulrich Gruenwald, a tall, muscular man with a nice suntan just like Sepp’s mother from working a lot outdoors. He was shaking Sepp’s hand: “Welcome young man. I have heard your parents are from Sudetenland! I am from Transylvania in Romania. My family was deported just like your family. We ended up in Schwaben, where I met the wife, my Ursula!” It was Ursula who asked: “How about some plum-cake and a glass of fresh milk?” Sepp couldn’t say no! She watched him nodding his head and got busy bringing out plates, forks and a sheet with the still warm cake. She asked him to sit down as she put a big helping of plum-cake on his plate. She poured him milk: “Fresh from the cow!” she said, and Ulrich confirmed it: “Just before you got here, I finished milking the cows!” It was a good cake, sweet with a hint of tartness. Ursula and Ulrich had joined him. Herr Gruenwald was praising the cooking and baking qualities of his wife. She started with: “You know about Mel?” The looks on Sepp’s face were enough of an answer, aside from him shaking his head. Ursula continued: “Mel is back in Cologne with my parents, Kleinerort just wasn’t right for him. See after you left Herr Hauptlehrer Meyer’s school, Mel told us that he had nobody who wanted to have anything to do with him. Mel said they asked him about the meaning of Mel. Therefore he explained to the other kids his name, the being named after King Melchior. The kids made fun of him. They were calling him all kind of names. Kid’s can be so cruel! Mel was discouraged by the insults and finally refused going back to Hauptlehrer Meyer’s school!”

To change the subject, Herr Gruenwald asked: “Do you know anyone in Kleinerort who would want to help in the fields? As you know the Neuhof is not our farm. It belongs to some rich folks, and they pay well for hourly labor!” “Ja! I will ask my mother!” Sepp answered. Soon after, he left the farm and Sepp was sad because here he had had a friend, but now Mel was gone. He had left him, for the big city somewhere far away!

At age ten Sepp's 'Firmung' (Confirmation) was in a medieval town about 20 kilometers from home. It was in a Rococo and Gothic style Catholic Church, founded in 724AD, first documented in 1329, but most likely older. Many of the sculptures were by Reuss and Riemenschneider. The Confirmation in the Roman Catholic Church was supposed to make Sepp a full-fledged member of the Catholic Church. He had been baptized in Kitzingen and had his First Communion in Hinterberg. He had done his service as an altar boy. Here now supposedly Sepp was getting to know the holy ghost according to the scriptures: *"Now when the apostles, who were in Jerusalem, had heard that Samaria had received the word of God, they sent unto them Peter and John. Who, when they were come down, prayed for them, that they might receive the Holy Ghost. For he was not as yet come upon any of them; but they were only baptized in the name of the Lord Jesus. Then they laid their hands upon them, and they received the Holy Ghost."*

Sepp was anxiously looking forward to the Firmung (Confirmation) because that's when boys or girls were getting their first watch, as it was the custom at the time. Yes, he too wanted to have his watch. Getting to know the Holy Ghost was okay, but always knowing the time of the day was a much more meaningful improvement for a boy like Sepp. It all turned into a saddening situation when Sepp found out that all those other kids got their watch, but none for him. The Schusters after paying for the taxi to the Firmung and everything else just didn't have the money to buy a watch for Sepp. How could they do that to him? Sepp was very disappointed. He was angry, tormented by feeling let down. He remembered not getting his watch for years to come. Yes to be on time in school, he knew the ring of the church bells, and how to tell time on any clear day. He was used to checking every clock tower on his way, for the right time. To have a wind-up pocket watch and being able to see the hour and minute day or night, it was what he had set his heart on, for quite some time now.

Every day in spring, summer, and the fall Sepp rode his bicycle, the fast 18-speed bike, from Kleinerort to the Oberrealschule in Unterschwarzenberg, and back home. In the winter months, his mother found Sepp a place to stay much closer to school. Erika wanted him to become an engineer, and she made sure that he could get to school. Looking back in later years, as far as Sepp could remember, he had never missed a class. Sepp did see Ulrich a few times as Waldemar repaired shoes and boots for the Gruenwald family and Erika occasionally worked for the Neuhof farm too. She praised them for being very nice people. Erika greatly appreciated getting an exceptional good pay per hour worked, much better than she had ever been paid working in the fields. Sepp knew that his mother worked hard to allow him to stay in school and have the best possible education. He liked going to school. Sepp always wanted to learn new things, and his grades showed it.

It was in Unterschwarzenberg where he met a boy, one-year-older than Sepp. He was a head taller too. Straight dark blond hair covered his ears and part of his neck. His haircut was considered long in the 1960s. The boy's friendly "Where are you from? Haven't seen you here before!" received a "Ja! Kleinerort, I go to school here now! Oberrealschule, you know!" "So! Are you one of those snobbish kids?" the boy questioned him. A perplexed Sepp just looked at him, because he didn't know the meaning of snobbish. Then somewhat flustered, he said: "My parents are from Sudetenland, my father is a shoemaker, and my mother works helping the farmers in Kleinerort. I am Sepp Schuster!" The boy grabbed Sepp's hand saying "Look! I am Eddie. I am born here in Unterschwarzenberg. Want me to show you around?" with that and his "Ja! Yes!" Sepp started to hang out with Eddie, whenever time allowed.

Over the summer break from school, middle of July to end of August 1961, Sepp got an invitation to visit his father's daughter from first marriage, Edeltraud. Everybody called her Traude. Sepp had never met her, but surely enjoyed all the presents she had been sending him over the years. Sepp was overjoyed. He had never been on an airplane before, and now he got to fly by himself from Nuremberg to West Berlin. It was all arranged and paid for by Traude Schuster. Waldemar organized a ride for Sepp to the airport in Nuremberg with a leather salesman who was driving back to his leather and hides supply house in Fuerth near Nuremberg. It was Sepp's first trip to a big city. The salesman was a large fellow who talked a lot. He dropped Sepp and his rucksack off, in the parking lot, at the airport in Nuremberg.

Here Sepp stood on the sidewalk in front of an enormous building. Sepp was uncertain as to where to go now. Challenged but hopeful Sepp approached an older couple “Gruess Gott! Ja, I am Sepp Schuster. I am going to fly to Berlin, to see my sister Traude. Where is my airplane?” The woman laughed, and the man asked Sepp to follow as they walked him to the airport entrance and pointed him in the direction of the airline’s information center. Listening to Sepp’s “Danke schoen!” they answered with what sounded to Sepp like “Hatsloche un Broche!”

Once Sepp approached the airline counter, one lady, who apparently was expecting him, asked: “Gruess Gott, young man, are you the

Sepp Schuster we are waiting for?" "Ja! Yes, and I am looking for my airplane. I am going to fly to Berlin to see my sister Traude!" he answered. She grabbed some tickets, and said "Sepp, please come with me!" and accompanied him to the plane. The plane was not full. Here Sepp was allowed to sit next to a little window. It wasn't long before the aircraft took off. Looking out the window and down, there was not much to see, most of the trip they were in or above the clouds. Sepp was comfortable, after all, he had no idea what to expect. The two engines were very noisy. Sepp liked the lady who gave him his first CocaCola. It tasted funny, but because it was an American drink, it was a special treat. It was bubbly, somewhat sweet. He liked it just because it was something new and it was CocaCola. The stewardess told him to relax as they got ready to approach the airport in Berlin. It was a short flight, less than an hour. The kindhearted woman was telling him about the plane and Berlin. She also helped him to undo his seatbelt after they arrived in Tempelhof.

Traude was waiting for him at the airport Berlin Tempelhof. She looked somewhat like the woman in the picture, the one his father had given Sepp before he left, but older. Sepp showed her the photo, and Traude remembered that it had been taken years ago when she was in her late 30s. Traude insisted on carrying his rucksack for him. He let her. They took a bus to Berlin Reinickendorf. Sepp had never before been on a bus. From the bus stop it was a short walk to her apartment building. Here they stepped through a door into a box with buttons on the wall. Sepp had never been in an elevator either. Traude noticed and explained: "Taking the elevator is much faster than going up the stairs!" Sepp was impressed. Traude’s apartment was filled with new looking old fashioned furnishings. Hand embroidered table toppers and table covers were everywhere. She also had a television-set and a big radio and a reel-to-reel player and a record-player, as well as a telephone. All those techno-gadgets were new to Sepp because they didn't have any of these in Kleinerort. Traude showed him one of the records and explained, “I am borrowing these round disks called ‘Schallplatten’ from my friends and record the same on the tape to play back later!” while he admired her reel-to-reel recording machine. Sepp was fascinated by the moving pictures in black and white on the tube, what she called television-set.

Traude was on vacation, instead of going away, she had made plans to have her little brother come and visit. She was all prepared to show young Sepp her city, to show him her Berlin. That evening, just before sending Sepp to bed, Bertha, her neighbor came by for a 'Klatsch' and a nightcap. Traude introduced Sepp to her. Both Traude and Bertha used to work together, until recently. Bertha had retired from working as a nurse last month. The two women uncorked a bottle of wine and talked about the exciting events in their lives while Sepp got ready for bed. Sepp's head was filled with all the adventures of the day, the plane ride, the CocaCola, the big city, the bus, the elevator, and the electronics in Traude's place. He dreamed a lot.

The next day Traude took Sepp to the Berliner Zoo located in the southwest portion of the Tiergarten, a public park. Here he got to see many species of the animal world from around the planet, including two pandas, four wolves, a rhinoceros, gorillas, two elephants, two lions, one tiger and so much more. Sepp had never seen such a variety of exotic animals. He was delighted and asked eagerly “How come you have so many different animals here in your town? We have only foxes, deer, cats, dogs, horses, cows and goats where I live!” Traude laughed and assured Sepp that those animals aren’t native to Berlin and that “A zoo is the collection of wild animals from around the world, to show visitors like us!” Traude and Sepp spent most of the day at the zoo. Here Traude bought him Berliner Bratwurst (sausage in a bun) and a Berliner Weisse, a cloudy, sour white beer with a shot of sweet syrup. Sepp was in heaven. He had to have a second Berliner Weisse.

On the way back they took the S-Bahn. They got off the train near the Spandau Prison. Standing there and looking at the red brick walls and towers of the prison-building, Traude explained: "Here they keep Rudolf Hess, locked up, as the only remaining prisoner from WWII, and he is watched by Russian, British, French and American guards rotating weekly." Sepp’s spontaneous question, “Ja! Traude please can we go in and watch him too?” made Traude laugh, “No, we don’t want to!” she said. Sepp asked “Ja! You say Rudolf Hess is so dangerous, we can’t see him, and they need soldiers from four countries to make sure he can’t escape?” Traude laughed again “No! But you are right he is the only prisoner, and there are lots of soldiers guarding him!” Later at home Traude told Sepp what she knew about Rudolf Hess, about his flight to Scotland, the becoming a POW in Britain in 1941. Traude talked about Rudolf Hess’s mental issues and without having had much if any say whatsoever in Hitler’s war, in 1945 he was imprisoned for life in Spandau.

"East-Berlin, as you know, is in the Russian sector," Traude explained, "Reinickendorf is in the French sector!" and added, "Other sectors are the American and the British sector." The next day they went back to the Tiergarten, to see the Brandenburger Tor and the Victory Column. Traude also showed him the Bellevue Palace and the House of World Cultures built in 1957 by the United States as part of an architectural exhibition and show. Traude referred to it as the “Alter Weiber Hut” (resembling a hat style worn by old women).

In the S-Bahn, one lovely older lady asked Traude if she would ‘bitte-bitte-bitte’ help her and exchange some money for her. Traude nodding her head exchanged 20 marks in coins. After the lady had gotten off the train at the next station, Traude showed Sepp the money she had received. It was East German, DDR money, made from aluminum. She explained: "That is hard-earned money in East Berlin, useless over here in the West. So if she wants to buy any food, anything in West Berlin, she needs BRD (West German) money and not DDR (East German) money." That was also the time when Traude explained to Sepp that the S-Bahn served both parts of Berlin, West Berlin and East Berlin, the Soviet sector.

It wasn't until the third day staying with Traude that an inquisitive Sepp asked her about Dr. Sauerbruch because he knew from his father that his daughter used to work directly with the world-famous doctor. Sepp had heard that Dr. Sauerbruch had invented the Sauerbruch-chamber and that he had created artificial limbs. He had been rewarded with several medals for his research. Sepp knew from his father that there was a film made about Dr. Ferdinand

Sauerbruch's and life and work. Traude talked to Sepp about Ferdinand, the doctor and that he was the reason she worked at the Charité in the first place. Sepp wanted to know what happened to the Charité hospital. Sepp knew that Traude, Waldemar's daughter from his first wife, had been in Berlin when the Russian soldiers took over. And Traude told him that she had refused to leave Berlin when Waldemar came for her about a week or two before the war ended. "When a bomb destroyed the east wing, we all thought it was an error. Later when another bomb destroyed the big lecture hall, we still thought it was an error. Because of the Geneva Conventions and hospitals are supposed to be safety zones, we all had high hopes that we shall be in the clear. It was not so! During the last days of the war, in and around the hospital saw heavy house-to-house fighting. Wherever you looked the still standing walls showed bullet holes."

A nosy Sepp kept on poking. He wanted to know more. He asked questions about Berlin in 1945. But he never got to hear the full story about Traude's personal life during the Russian occupation. She just didn't want to talk about it.

The next day, as Traude had a doctor appointment, she left Sepp in her neighbor's care. To be with Bertha was fun. She fed him cheesecake on strawberry puree and hot chocolate. Bartha was sipping pink wine from a tall stem glass and asked questions about school and Kleinerort. Bertha told him about her having worked together with Traude Schuster since the day when Traude showed up at the Charité. Bertha was proud to have worked at the Charité, built in 1710. And she raved about Traude: "Your sister is an excellent nurse and one of the finest human beings on earth!" Bertha talked about Traude's being close friends with Dr. Ferdinand Sauerbruch, aside from being engaged to Dr. Steiner, Dr. Sauerbruch's right hand. "It was a shame when he lost his life in 45! Dr. Steiner was an excellent surgeon and a frank and honest, genuine decent, responsible person with very admirable traits!"

Sepp asked Bertha more questions to get a better picture of what happened once the Russian troops took possession of the hospital. Bertha told him: "By the end of the war, there were very few men left in Berlin. The Russian soldiers had not only permission but had orders to brutally use and abuse any German women they found. And nurses are women too!" Then she added: "And your Traude was also one of the unlucky ones as she looked like the kind of woman the Russian soldiers' had expected to find as their carnal booty!" That was pretty much all Bertha told him. Later in the day after Traude came back, Sepp asked Traude if Bertha's stories were true. Traude answered: "If my neighbor and friend Bertha said so, it must be true!" Sepp wanted to know: "Ja! What does it mean? Carnal booty?" "Earthly goods!" she answered.

To the question: "Ja! What happened to Dr. Steiner, why didn't you get married?" Traude didn't want to talk about, just changed the subject.

The days with Traude went fast. Some days Sepp went off on his own, to explore the city. He had no problem finding his way back. One place he liked a lot was the KaDeWe, the Kaufhaus Des Westens, a huge department store. Sepp was overwhelmed by the variety of goods on display. He hadn't seen anything like it before. And there was so much to explore, a brand new world for him. Traude was quite concerned because Sepp was riding on the S-Bahn in East Berlin when the Russian occupying forces closed the Brandenburger Tor in August of 1961. The day before leaving West Berlin Traude went with him to the KaDeWe, and she bought him a suitcase. The next day he departed with the rucksack on his back and the small suitcase filled with gifts from Traude. She delivered him to the airport. The airplane was bigger than the one he came on. Sepp's mind was busy. He wondered how to get to the train station in Nuremberg once he arrived at the airport. "Maybe I just walk there?" He thought, knowing once he found his way to the Bahnhof, the rest was going to be easy. All he had to do was buy a ticket and get on the train to Kitzingen. The stewardess was taking good care of him on the short trip, and after he had told her that he needs to get a train to Kitzingen, and then take the bus home. She asked: "Is anyone expecting you in Kitzingen?" His answer was "Ja! No! Nobody. At home, we have no phone, and they don't know that I am coming home today! They do know that I planned to be back before school starts, next week." The woman's name was Frau

Freundlich, and as he got off the plane, she told him: "Don't leave the airport but wait at the end of the tarmac at the door to the airport arrival area." He did as told. Sepp liked Frau Freundlich, who had fed him two Salz Brezels aside the CocaCola. By now he was a seasoned airplane traveler and therefore expected to get CocaCola anytime.

After all the passengers had gotten off the plane, finally, Frau Freundlich carrying a small suitcase and a piece of paper in hand showed up, and she asked Sepp to follow her. Inside the building at a counter, she had to make a phone call. As she was talking to whomever at the other side, she looked at Sepp and mentioned his name several times. She also said: "Bernd and I will be driving down to Kitzingen tomorrow morning. We have plenty of space in the car. If you give your permission, your little brother can stay with us, and we take him right home to Kleinerort in the morning." Then she handed Sepp the phone. He had never used a phone before, so Sepp needed a little help to figure out where the mouthpiece was and what side to hold against his ear. It was Traude on the phone. Not only had she arranged the flight, but she also had requested to be called once he had landed safely in Nuremberg. Traude told him: “Be a guter Junge, Frau Freundlich and her husband shall drive you home tomorrow morning. You don’t need to look for a train or bus. She will take care of everything!” Sepp did say: “Ja! Dankeschoen Traude, die Frau Freundlich ist sehr nett zu mir!” He didn’t know what else to say and gave the phone receiver back. He heard her telling Traude: “No you don’t have to pay us, to take your little brother home. Kleinerort is not out of our way!”

Sepp had the feeling Traude liked him. She had never married, and she had no children. Sepp liked her a lot, because she was so good to him.

A receptive Sepp followed Frau Freundlich leaving the airport building to a car waiting for her. A nice man, Frau Freundlich’s age, opened the door for her, he asked: “Whom do we have here?” She introduced all: “This is Bernd, my husband, and please call me Elisabeth!” looking at Sepp, “Sepp is staying with us overnight. I promised his sister in Berlin that we shall drop him off in Kleinerort tomorrow morning on our trip to Kitzingen!" "Oh ein Berliner?" Bernd asked. "No, his parents are Sudeten Deutsche, and he grew up in Kleinerort, it was his very first trip to a big city!" Elisabeth corrected him. Bernd asked, "Sepp have you ever been in Nuremberg?" "Ja! Yes, when I was dropped off here in front of the airport!" Sepp answered. "But have you seen the town, the castle?" Sepp was shaking his head. Bernd asked his wife: "You have any plans for the afternoon?" When she answered, "Nein!" Bernd suggested, "Let's take Sepp to the Imperial Castle before we go home!"

Bernd knew his way around town. Below the castle, he parked in a side street, and they walked over a bridge to a large open-air market in front of an old church. Here Bernd bought lunch for everyone 'Nuremberger Bratwuerstle Drei Im Weggla (three in a bun).' These were good sausages. They had packed three small pork sausages in a roll, and the mustard was just right too. With it, they had a side dish of cabbage. To drink all three had a 'Spritzer' consisting of wine diluted with carbonated water. Bernd also got an order of 'Presssack mit Musik' (headcheese with music) for all to try. Sepp's question "Ja! Where is the music?" had both, Bernd and Elisabeth, laughing. She tried to explain: "Music means with onion because they are flatulence!" Sepp's facial expression was a give-a-way, he had no idea what she meant with flatulence. Bernd said it: "With music means with onions, the word music refers to the trumpet sounds you may make when you fart, because of eating onions!" Now Sepp understood. He was laughing as he was eating the onion rings, all just because.

Done eating, they went on up to the castle. It was hard to miss. Any place looking up Sepp saw the symbol of the city of Nuremberg. Bernd didn't get tired to show Sepp up to and through the fortified buildings overlooking the city below. Once in the courtyard, Bernd was leading the way to the Heidenturm, the Emperors Chapel, the Deep Well, Sinwell Tower and the Luginsland Tower. A keen, enthusiastic Sepp enjoyed the view down, seeing all of Old Town from above. "The castle was another place Friedrich Barbarossa used to stay!" according to Bernd. "All the Emperors of the Holy Roman Empire have stayed at one time or the other here at the Imperial Castle!" Then Bernd went on to talk about several noble families and

Emperors while Sepp busy looking didn't hear much until Bernd brought up a famous character: "Around the 1370s they were holding Eppelein von Geilingen, the Franconian robber here at the Castle in a cell."

"Because Eppelein von Geilingen had been robbing merchants traveling to and from Nuremberg successfully for many years, he was going to be hanged from the neck. On the day of his hanging, his last wish was to sit one last time on his beloved horse. The planned hanging was happening within the walls of the castle. All the gates were closed. There was no way to ride out. Therefore his wish was granted. And Eppelein got on his horse, and rode his horse up onto the walkway of the wall, from where he forced the horse into a gallop before jumping from high up over the moat." And Bernd showed Sepp a hoof print: "That's where Eppelein's horse jumped off." Sepp wanted to know: "Ja! What happened to Eppelein?" Elisabeth who had quietly followed the two added: "Some say he went down to your area, and build several towers near Kleinerort where he kept on robbing merchants as they came through!" Bernd let him know: “Eppelein became a folk hero and therefore shall live on forever!”

There was so much more to see in the Nuremberg castle. It was in the late afternoon that they left. Bernd drove to an area with new homes, here they, Elizabeth and Bernd lived in a three-bedroom house. The furnishing was very modern, and everything looked and smelled new. Elisabeth explained: “We just moved into the house! We are both from Kitzingen. Our families live there!”

Sepp slept well in the new bed, in a new place, and all he dreamed of was that Eppelein von Geilingen. The next morning after breakfast, consisting of bread, marmalade, hard-boiled egg, and milk with a dash of chocolate, they took off on their trip to Kleinerort. In the car, Bernd was telling Sepp some stories about the Nuremberger Funnel, which supposedly allowed wisdom to be poured directly in the students’ brains. Bernd had Sepp laughing as he told jokes. And Sepp was listening to Bernd explaining the importance of Nuremberg over the ages: “In the years of 1945 to 1946 the city was the place for the Nuremberg trials. 1933 to 1938 it was the site for huge, real huge Nazi Party conventions. The first German railway, the Bavarian Ludwigsbahn started here in 1835. Back in 1500AD, Nuremberg was the Centre of German Renaissance. And yes the city of Nuremberg is also known as the 'unofficial capital' of The Holy Roman Empire."

Before he knew it, they arrived in Kleinerort. The 2-hour drive in Bernd's comfortable car flew by so fast. Elisabeth delivered Sepp into the hands of his mother, who was happy to see her son returning from the big city. Erika tried to give Bernd some money for gasoline. He refused. Erika grabbed a home smoked Schinken fresh from the smoker and that one they couldn't refuse. After Elizabeth and Bernd had left, Waldemar asked: "Where did you find those exceptional people? Being chauffeured in a Benz limousine, you are getting around young man!" "Jawohl our Sepp is living it up, hanging out with rich folks!" Erika added.

Here Sepp was telling his parents about his trip: "Ja! I had CocaCola, three times now. The Brezels on the plane are not as good as Anita's. Traude said they change guards at the Spandau

Prison every week. And I know where Eppelein von Geilingen escaped from, before settling here near Kleinerort in one of these castles. And in Nuremberg, they are serving Presssack mit Musik!" And both were smiling, Erika and Waldemar realized their Sepp had a wonderful time.

Sepp hadn't realized that Herr and Frau Freundlich had a unique car, it was big, but what did he know, aside from that those two were real nice people. Two weeks later, in a letter, Traude asked Sepp about the visit with the 'Van DeLichte' family was. Now Sepp realized that because of the airplane noise he didn't hear right, when Elisabeth said her name, so it wasn't Freundlich at all, but Van DeLichte.

Going back to school, he looked up Eddie, and they went roller-skating all over town. Eddie showed Sepp all the new development at the north end of Unterschwarzenberg. Here they were building a Shuhfabrik, a place where shoes were going to be made en-masse. And on the other side of town, the Schwimmbad (public swimming pools) was being enlarged. In the middle of the city, the movie theater was being renovated as well.

Eddie asked Sepp “Do you like soccer?” And he got an instant: “Ja! Oh ja! When? Where?” answer. “How about tomorrow after you get out of school? Meet us at the lake!” Next day, after class Sepp met Eddie and his friends, and they played soccer till late in the Afternoon. It was Eddie who suggested: “We need you in our team, you are fast, and you know how to kick the ball past the goalie!”

The following winter Sepp was put up, staying, in the Catholic Boys Boarding home right next to the Oberrealschule in Unterschwarzenberg. He learned to play Ping-Pong, and Sepp was getting real good with it too.

Sepp Schuster was a slender boy, now 149cm tall, weighing about 45kg. And Sepp enjoyed wearing his lederhosen every day, the Knickerbocker style deer leather pants. He knew how to give them some character by adding some patina. Not only did he clean his hands on the pants, but also quite frequently rubbed butter and oil into the leather, they started to look just right. His mother always cut his hair short. That winter he let it grow a little longer than usual.

While being at the Catholic Boys Boarding home, somebody was telling Sepp that Pope John XXIII had excommunicated Fidel Castro. Sepp had no idea who that Fidel Castro was. However, he understood that when the Pope, being the right hand of the Catholic God is mad at someone, it's very bad. Sepp didn't want to be excommunicated. Therefore Sepp asked himself the question "Ja! How am I going to make sure the Pope will never find out about my sinful life?" And what he was worried about was the going to confession and not always telling the whole truth.

In the afternoons when a group of students walked down to the lake to go ice-skating, Sepp was right there. He was good on his skates. Eddie was there too, with some of his buddies. Eddie seemed to know everybody in Unterschwarzenberg. Since the day when Eddie had asked Sepp to join the soccer team, whenever possible Sepp went to see Eddie, whose usual hangout was the lake and adjacent park. When Eddie asked Sepp to join and play ice hockey on Eddie's team, Sepp had the very best time he ever had with those boys. The Oberrealschule also had an ice hockey team, yet Sepp got to play against them as part of Eddie's team, which was representing the City School of Unterschwarzenberg. It was Eddie's team, which won.

The following spring, 12 years old, a reed-like boy, indestructible, riding his bike daily for hours, Sepp became the fastest 100-meter runner his school had ever witnessed. Sepp didn't run because of the competition, or to get a reward. For him, it was most important to prove a point, because he knew he could outrun the best, so he was going to show them all. Sepp had run the 100 meters in 10.2 seconds, several times before, nearly as fast as Armin Hary who did so in 10.1 seconds at the 1960 Olympic Games, a couple of years earlier. Some kids in school, who had heard about Sepp being faster than anyone else in his age-group had been accusing Sepp of making things saying, "You are just a braggart, you can't run so fast!" At the school sports competition, the instructors made him run twice, and still, both fellows with the stopwatches questioned the accuracy of the result. Hearing the "That can't be right" and "Something is wrong, nobody is so fast" Sepp didn't stay for the ceremony. He got on his bike and went riding the roads by himself like he always did. All he wanted was to be left alone. From that day on some kids called Sepp 'Flash.'

The same year during summer break, Sepp played soccer with Eddie and the boys. When Waldemar handed Sepp 200DM and asked him to go and see Munich, Sepp was delighted. He was looking forward to go and see Karl, his stepbrother. Sepp was all excited, since seeing Traude in Berlin this was Sepp's up and coming greatest adventure. Sepp told Eddie and all his friends that he was going to see Munich. Sepp was expecting nothing less inspiring than his visit with Traude the previous year in Berlin. Eddie said: "You are getting to see the world, you are a traveler! See you when you get back!"

Sepp got ready to meet his half-brother Karl Schuster in Munich. Sepp had all he needed to be packed in his rucksack. On Sunday early morning Sepp in his lederhosen rode his bicycle to the train station in Unterschwarzenberg. Here he locked his bike to the bike rack. Backpack in hand, he walked up to the ticket window and bought his return ticket to Munich. From the 200DM, Sepp still had a lot of money left over.

The train rolled in, came to a stop and Sepp got aboard the train for Munich. He found an empty compartment and settled down. It was a very large six-seat compartment, with heavy duty upholstered seats, very comfortable. Minutes after the train left the station, the ticket inspector came by and punched Sepp's ticket. With a warm, friendly voice he asked "Young man you travel by yourself? Is today the first time that you are riding the rain?" Sepp was surprised and admitted: "Ja! Yes, alone, jawohl first time!" The Bundesbahn gentleman in a sympathetic way offered "Let me show you all you need to know whenever you travel by train. Young man, I still remember my first train ride." He gave Sepp a short tour throughout the train. He showed Sepp where the bathrooms are, then where to get some food, the 'Speisewagen.' Later the conductor came back to check on

Sepp, and he promised: “I shall come by and let you know when we get closer to the Munich-West Bahnhof.” Sepp felt special, and as he knew where to get a drink, he went and bought himself a CocaCola. He looked and found the folded up envelope in his pocket, the envelope with Karl’s invitation. The sender address was Munich-West Oberdorfer Weg #13.

At the next stop his compartment filled up, he was no longer by himself. From here on he had company, a family of four. They were busy chatting and laughing and talking. Sepp did not understand one word. It was a foreign language. Certain words he thought he knew, as he was taking Latin in school. The ticket inspector kept his word: “Young man, we shall be in Munich-West, in less than ten minutes, time to get ready!” He even opened the door for Sepp, as the train came to a halt. Outside the train station, Sepp asked a bus driver: “Ja! Grüss Gott! Can you please tell me how I get to Oberdorfer Weg from here?” And the driver pointed down the road and said: “The bus going out there has just left, but it’s not far young man, it’s only 2 kilometers down the Haupstrasse and over the bridge, and then the first street on your right after the bridge, that's Oberdorfer Weg." Wearing proper 'Wanderschuhe,' Sepp was ready to go. He was thinking: "Ja! What do I need a bus, when I can walk?" And walking he did. Sepp had no problems to find his way to Oberdorfer Weg #13.

Karl's house was big, larger than the school house in Kleinerort. It was quite sizeable, capacious. Karl Schuster had a big family. He and his wife Doris had six children. In plain sight on the wall, there was a tiny little round button, the doorbell, which Sepp didn't see at first. As the front door was locked, he knocked and knocked, and nobody answered. Then giving up, he was leaning against the wall, and he heard the bell ringing. Only after turning around and looking at the real small whitish round button, and pressing it again did he realize that it wasn't a light-switch but a 'bell-switch.'

The door opened, a tall blond woman in her late thirties looked at him, and asked "You must be Sepp?" and Sepp was saying: "Ja, Grüss Gott!" and with an "I am Doris, please come in!" she asked Sepp to enter. As all of Karl's kids had come to the door, they caused a minor traffic snarl, and Sepp was busy saying to every one:

"Grüss Gott!" "Grüss Gott!" "Grüss Gott!" "Grüss Gott!" "Grüss Gott!" "Grüss Gott!" but there was no way for him to squeeze past those seven bodies in front of him. Then Karl showed up and with a "Kids make space, let your Uncle Sepp come in the house!" the traffic congestion at the door eased.

Karl was just as Waldemar had said. Karl was a younger version of Waldemar. They looked much the same. Their talking was different as Karl had a typical Bavarian accent. Karl took Sepp by the hand and led him through the house, then showed him to the guest room right next to the kitchen, where he told his younger brother: "Sepp that's your room while you are here, you can put your bag on the bed!" And so Sepp did, he left his rucksack on the bed. Sepp followed his stepbrother to the kitchen. Here Doris had her kids lined up, and she asked them: "Kids you need to tell Uncle Sepp your name and age!" The oldest started: "I am Kurt, and I am ten years old!" "I Rudi, am nine!" "Edeltraud and next to me is my twin sister Edelmarie we are seven years old!" "I am Waldo, and six, named after my grandfather Waldemar!" and last "Hugo, I am three!" It was

Kurt who let Sepp know: "Waldo, is only five, until his birthday next week!" Sepp was impressed, and before he could say anything, Karl addressed his kids and told them: "Doris and I have to go to work these next four days. So Kurt, Rudi, Hugo and Waldo it's your job to take care of our guest!" "What about us?" Edelmarie asked, and Karl said: "I want you both to keep an eye on your brothers, make sure the boys treat Uncle Sepp with respect, call me anytime if there is a problem!"

The same evening they all had dinner together, and Karl and Doris were asking many questions about Kleinerort, about Waldemar and his shoemaker business. Karl was talking about the Schuster Shoemaker Shop in Troppau, the yearly family get-together, a week-long party in Troppau, with more than 200 people of which over a hundred were close relatives. Then Karl talked about the clientele, the men and women of high importance the Schusters had had over the centuries. Somehow Karl couldn't understand that Waldemar living and working in a little 'Häusle' could be happy with fixing dirty old boots and shoes for two- dozen farmers in Kleinerort. When Sepp asked Karl "Ja! But when did you last visit father in Kleinerort?" Karl looked uncomfortable, "No, I haven't had time for a trip to Kleinerort!" And Doris said: "Karl you travel a lot for the company, maybe you should make time to see your father!" "Yes I do travel, but that's all for business!" he answered. That night Sepp slept deep in the big soft bed. Next morning all had breakfast together, consisting of one soft-boiled egg, served in an egg-cup, toast, and jam, milk for the kids and coffee for the grown-ups. Karl and Doris left for work just after all had eaten.

Sepp spent the day with Karl's kids at the house, and he got to see their toys and listened to the kids talking boastingly about all those things they had and their exciting lifestyle. They all had been to museums! Sepp didn't even know what a museum was. They all had been to theater shows! Sepp had no idea about theaters. They all had been to movies! Sepp knew where there was a movie theater in Unterschwarzenberg, but Sepp had never been in a movie theater.

"Are you saying you don't go to museums, theaters, or movies? What do you do in

Kleinerort?" Kurt asked. "Watch the cows pooping, and the grass grow!" Rudi said. And shamefaced Sepp was quietly listening.

They, Karl's kids were going swimming every so often! Sepp had never gone swimming, not counting breaking through the ice and falling into the lake in Unterschwarzenberg. Sepp realized that Karl's kids had done so much, while he, Sepp had done so little. Then Waldo showed him his FM/AM radio. Kurt pointed out that each kid had a radio in their room! Sepp had none. They each also had a portable radio. Sepp had none. They also had a television-set in two different rooms, one for the parents, and the other for the kids. Sepp's parents didn't have one at home. "You have no television?" Marie asked, and both girls Edelmarie and Edeltraude giggled. They each had their very own room! At home Sepp slept in the same room with his mother and Frieda if she was home, only Waldemar had his very own room. Then Rudi showed Sepp the phone system, which allowed him to make a call to anyone of his brothers and sisters rooms, or to his parents, by just pressing a number. Sepp had never seen anything like it. He thought phone calls were always made to a switchboard operator who puts you through to whatever number you wish to call. At Karl's home, they had not just one phone, but also a direct dial phone system. Every kid's room had its very own phone. Sepp's home had none.

"Are you saying, that you don't have your very own room?" Rudi asked. "Ja! We have one big bedroom with three beds in it!" "It must be a small house, then!" Rudi said. "Ja! Why do you have so many radios and phones and televisions, how come?" Sepp wanted to know. Karl's oldest son, Kurt, one year younger than Sepp, explained: "My dad works for an electronic and technology company. Just like you have better shoes, we have the better technology." When Sepp mentioned he would like to trade shoes for some of the kid's technology, the answer was laughter. All of Karl's kids laughed and laughed. A stupefied Sepp wasn't too sure why. Waldo's "How can he be so stupid?" was adding more laughter. Karl's kids were all younger than Sepp. They also were so much smarter than Sepp, and they succeeded to make sure he would never forget it.

Doris was home by 3 and Karl got home around 6 o'clock. Again they all had dinner together, and it was Sepp who after being tormented by his brother's kids all day was doing his part to make sure they all knew he had been traveling and seen something. Sepp talked about last year when he was in Berlin: "Traude took me to the Zoo, and she let me ride the S-Bahn by myself. On the plane, I got to drink CocaCola and eat Brezels, and when I visited the Imperial Castle we had 'Presssack mit Musik,' I had a great time flying by myself to Berlin and visiting all of Nuremberg with Elisabeth and Bernd."

When Karl asked "What do you think about our sister Traude?" "Ja! I like her a lot. Ja! I know she likes me too!" Sepp answered. "She has been sending me gifts, a bicycle, a sled, and many things. I like her very much!" And Sepp overheard Kurt talking to his brothers: "Traude, she has never sent us gifts! How can she do such to us?"

Soon it was bed time for the kids. Sepp was in bed, in the guest room, next to the kitchen. He couldn't sleep, his mind was too busy. Hadn't he come to Munich to have fun, to see the

Sepp's Epic Perils & Pitfalls by helmut s.

Plot: This story is epic in size. The tales of Sepp's growing up and searching for the place to call home spans continents. Each of the seven books is a complete story by itself. A smorgasbord of gourmet anecdotes, sexual adventures and their emotional and mystical angles are unique for each stage

Prose: The Sepp novels by helmut s. feature deep insights int the world of International hospitality, for both the front and the back of the house. The reader will be captivated by the prose all well seasoned with matter-of-fact commonplace vocabular and restaurant menu specific language as found plentiful throughout the episodes.

Originality: It is the story of resettled Germans after WWII. They are raising a boy named Sepp in Franconia. He become a man in the attic of a 1000-year-old restaurant in Hamburg, then experiences apartheid in South Africa, before discoverin the United States. This is not just another addict doing geographical moves, it's Sepp getting to know the world en route to his destiny. There is more to the saga than the secrecy around the father Sepp never knew, about his "Guardian Angel" and the rationale behind Sepp's spiritual an financial bankruptcies and suicidal attempts.

Character Development: This character-driven story masterfully defines individuals on many levels: physical descriptions, personality traits, and flaws. All the characters are well developed.

Blurb: This epic saga is cleverly composed with depth, wit, an breadth

by helmut s.

sights, to get to know the big city, to see stores and whatever there was to see? Sepp didn't come here to be put down by Karl's kids, because he didn't have what they had, and he was not as smart as them. Being still awake at a late hour he was listening in, unknown to them, to a conversation Karl had with his wife, Doris, about Traude, his sister.

Doris asked Karl, "I think your sister would have been a good mother! Why did she never tie the knot?" Karl answered "Traude had planned to get married. Her husband to be, he was shot in 45, by Russian soldiers, about a month short of the wedding day!" "Wasn't he the Doctor under Dr. Sauerbruch at the Charité?" Doris asked. Karl said, "That Sauerbruch he was one of those who used any number of prisoners from the camps, for medical test and experiments. I am not too fond of him!" Then Karl added: "Yes, the Russians killed Dr. Steiner. At the hospital, Steiner walked in on a group of Russian soldiers in the act of brutally raping his future wife. Steiner tried to get her out of there. That got him killed!" "How you know?" Doris inquired. "A nurse who had worked with Traude at the hospital told me, the same nurse who later looked after my sister when she recuperated from the injuries, caused by being abducted from the Charité and being forced to entertain a group of Russian officers for several days." "So that's why she doesn't want to talk about it! I see! How did you find that nurse?" Doris wanted to know. "If you have to know, it's Susanne, the sweet older nurse at our hospital where you gave birth to four of our kids," Karl answered. Doris was apparently surprised, yet Karl explained that because of their same last name, and being from Troppau, in the Sudetenland, Susanne had asked if he was a relative of a woman by the name of Traude Schuster, the one she knew from way back when she was working at the Charité too. Here Karl did ask his wife not to talk to the kids or Traude about what he just said, because the last thing his sister needed was getting hurt, by opening old wounds and reliving the past.

From what he had just heard, Sepp gathered that the reason Traude never had any children, had to do with the end of the war and the Russian invasion. Sepp just 12 years old understood but didn't fully comprehend. "Because of what the Russian soldiers had done with and to Traude, she never got married and therefore had no kids of her own!"

Sepp, with the rucksack on his back, left the next morning just after breakfast. Kurt was looking at him on the way out, with a questioning face and asked: "Are you leaving?" Sepp answered: "Ja, I need to leave. I am going to soccer practice, with my friend Eddie!"

Sepp got to the bus stop, and a bus pulled in. "Ja! Grüss Gott! Please tell me! Is this bus going to the Munich-West train station?" he asked the driver, and getting a "Yes come on board!" Sepp took the bus to the train station. Here he got on the first train going his direction, which was twenty minutes later. However it wasn't as luxurious as the other time, and it was not as fast a train, that one was a 'Bummelzug' the kind of train, which stops at every station. What had taken two and a half hours on Sunday, took now seven hours. But did it matter? On the train back home, Sepp was comparing his life with Karl's kids, and even they had more toys, more gadgets, he felt his life was somehow better, less noisy. During the time with Karl's family, neither Karl nor Doris had time for him, both were busy working all day. They were nice, the food was good, but Sepp was glad to be on the train going home. One more day in the same house with those little braggarts showing off their toys, those apparently wise young ones, would have been utterly intolerable. Yes! And Sepp was glad he didn't get into a fist fight with Karl's kids, most likely he would have been the loser against 6 of them anyhow.

Sepp arrived back in Unterschwarzenberg in the late afternoon. His bike was still there. Before riding home, he went to see Eddie. After telling his friend about the short visit in Munich and that he doesn't like his relatives because they were noisy braggadocios, Eddie asked him to stay overnight, what Sepp gladly did. Both didn't have to go to school, several weeks of school summer vacation was still ahead. In the morning Eddie's mother was feeding the boys before they adventured out, around town on roller skates. In the afternoon they played soccer. Sepp spent one more night at Eddie's home before pedaling back to Kleinerort. He was happy, and after an outstanding visit with friends and relatives, whereby the time spent with Eddie was the highlight, it was time to get back to his parents.

Sepp's father was surprised to see Sepp coming home much sooner than expected, yet he understood. Desperately looking for his pocket knife, the one he had gotten from Traude, Sepp emptied his rucksack on the floor, and it was Waldemar who spotted it first. Sepp was happy. When Sepp realized he had still a lot of money left from the 200DM Waldemar had given him, he made plans to buy books, to read about all those places he was going to visit, in the future.

In the week after Sepp had returned from Munich, Waldemar got a letter from Karl, asking if Sepp had brought home some electronic toys, toys belonging to Karl's kids, toys Sepp had stolen. Karl's father was not happy at all, yet Waldemar did believe Sepp, he knew Sepp had not brought anything back with him.

What a week? Erika had a good reason for celebration! She had opened a letter from the Red Cross stating: "We have located your sister

Heidi Bauer in Austria." It was the day Erika had been waiting for since 1945. Yes! The Red Cross had located her sister Heidi in Austria. Sepp hearing about Aunt Heidi was asking his mother: "Ja! What about the rest of your Sudetenland family, your brothers, my Uncles?" Erika was shaking her head, "Still no word from them, I also don't know what had happened to our parents and the whereabouts of my younger sister Olga!" Sepp wanted to know "Ja! What about the rest of the Bauer family and all your relatives?" Erika answered with a sorrowful voice "My Sepp, I just don't know!" But there was the news about Heidi. Sepp had an aunt, still alive, someone, who would be able to tell him more about what home used to be like in Sudetenland. Everyone was looking forward to Heidi's arrival and staying with her sister Erika. Sepp didn't fully understand at first why it had taken so long for the Red Cross to find her. Then he figured it out, communication per mail, took its time, and telephone service was still unreliable.

"And yes how true! Ja! In the early 1960s, we didn't have email, the Internet, no FaceTime, no Skype, no Twitter either."

“Ja! Why did his parents leave the homes of their ancestors to come to Kleinerort, the tiny village in Frankenland?” was the puzzling question lingering on in Sepp’s mind. He was trying to get a better knowledge of the Sudetenland. Therefore Sepp asked a lot of questions. The answers he got were all bits and pieces, and Sepp much discombobulated, slowly arranged the fragments to get a view of the at the time still very fuzzy picture. It took a while until Sepp’s mother provided some insights into those days in 1945 which ended with her getting deported from her ‘Heimat!’ According to her, “I am the lucky one! Too many Germans, people with German names and or because they spoke German got beaten to death, hanged, drowned or their throats slashed.”

Erika reflected back: “It all started out with the victorious Russian army, then there were those who were following in the wake of the Russian military, virtually none of them had any sympathy for anyone German. Some of them hated all Germans. Often a rope would do it, men or women, children or old persons died that way. Others, before unaffected by German actions, they too joined the stick-it-to-all-German-folk mob activities. Attitudes of doing with them Germans as you wish, kill if you want, just because and as an exemplification ended the life for many fine German-speaking families in Sudetenland. And yes! The Nazis were to blame for all sufferings the Jewish, Russian, Pole, Slav, Roma and Czech population had had to endure. So it is understandable that the mob felt to have the right to have us Germans suffer one way or the other. According to the Allied war propaganda, all Germans were able to do the utmost cruel and inhumanly deeds. Therefore they needed to be eradicated, and if not possible then at least decimated, the numbers decreased and controlled!"

"You and Waldemar were Nazis?" Sepp asked his mother, who answered: "I have never asked your father, but believe me, my son, I was no member of the National Socialist German Workers' Party! We were farmers. My parents were farmers. My grandparents farmed the land, so did my grand-grandparents." Then she explained that the Nazi Party had started in the 1920s in Germany. The same Party created the

Third Reich. The Nazi Party arrived in Sudetenland in 1938 and lasted until 1945, the end of World War II."

Sepp's mother tried to make Sepp understand that 'being at war' is not a nice place to be. "The sad part is that on all sides the ordinary people pay the price for political blunders and lack of diplomacy, our family too, has suffered a lot because of decisions made by those who misused their powers!" Yes, Sepp listened, because he wanted to know, yet it took a long, very long time until Sepp understood what his mother was saying. Erika talked to Sepp more about her sister Heidi, "I remember quite well how Heidi had handled those German soldiers when they arrived in Sudetenland. Heidi coming back from the dances she went to with the local SS groups talked about the men she had met. 'They are all just big boys,' she said. I also distinctly recall how Heidi had dealt with the Russian soldiers when they first got to our farm. My sister, she dealt with men like they were boys, and she knew how to play with them. Believe me, Sepp; there is no man born yet, whom Heidi couldn't handle. Over the years I have prayed a lot. It's a miracle, Heidi is coming here." With tears in her eyes, Erika said: "I couldn't do anything when I watched Heidi being thrown on the truck, which had come to take whatever goods these thieves found worth stealing. Never mind that they stole all the smoked meat left in the locker above the kitchen, all our sharp knives, many of our big pots, and all hand tools they could find, the axes and hammers, pliers and screwdrivers, wrenches and saws. I was helpless, incapable of keeping my sister. I saw the handful of men, waiting on the truck, as two of them were grabbing Heidi and passed her on to the others. Heidi was not going anywhere, but with them. There was nothing that would have stopped those who felt entitled to take possession of anyone German-speaking and any property owned by any German-speaking individual. They had left me on the farm because I was sick, real sick. I got over the cold by cooking onions, eating them and drinking the tea for days."

It was a few days later that Sepp because he kept on asking questions, was told more about what had happened in 1945. Erika still wondered about not having heard from any of her relatives: "Why haven't I gotten any information about my younger sister's whereabouts? Olga was the smartest kid in the family. About the time of the end of the war Olga left on horseback to the village to take a bag with smoked meat to her boyfriend's home, but she never came back. Then both my brothers they were in the Wehrmacht, as far I know they were last seen fighting on the Eastern Front. Sepp, see your grandparents, my parents, they were in Prague. They were visiting with relatives, just about the time of the so-called 'Prague Uprising,' by other name known as 'Hell on Earth.' Both your grandparents Lorenz and Marta Bauer never returned to our farm."

When Sepp asked Waldemar, his father, "What about your family, relatives and coworkers and friends left behind in Sudetenland?" The answer was, "Force majeure! If they are still alive, we shall hear from them, sooner or later, it's out of our control. Greater powers are in charge!"

These days now Sepp's mother was euphoric, and yes never mind that the Red Cross had located her older sister in an Insane Asylum in Austria. Yes, in an Insane Asylum, that's where she was for the past seven years, yet still, Erika was thrilled, to know, that her sister was alive.

Sepp cerebrated, spending much thought on how to find out where the gravesites of his Grand Parents are, or what happened to those uncles and aunts he had never met? Yes, Sepp had heard stories about German bodies being piled up along the streets of Prague, is that where the grandparents ended up 'in a mass-grave?' Sepp knew he would never get all the answers to his questions, yet he was intrigued by the thought of shedding some light on the mystery of his origin and family background. What about his mother's younger sister, what about Olga, did she pass through one of those 1215 (officially reported in the Czech Republic) internment camps, from where more than 100.000 people perished. These internment camps were in addition to 846 forced labor 'disciplinary centers' and more than 200 prisons all known to house German-speaking Sudetendeutsche, all known to abominable feed and maltreat those incarcerated, including juveniles, children, women, and men. Why had

Olga's horse not found its way home? Who killed the horse? Had it been slaughtered and eaten?

Yes, and Sepp knew that his father had not heard a word from his sister and the two brothers. The same was true for Rudolf, Waldemar's dad, Sepp's grandfather. Yes, Waldemar had not heard one word from any of his relatives. As far as Sepp knew, Waldemar came from a large family, at the yearly gatherings there were always more than a hundred family members present.

They all were waiting for Erika's sister to arrive. Looking forward to meeting his Aunt Heidi, Sepp somewhat understood his mother who said: "After Heidi was in 1945 forcefully taken from my side, I was panicking! I was uncertain as to what to do. No! I was not easily scared. But I was terrified as to what might happen to my sister. So I prayed! And see my prayers are answered, she is coming home!"

As there was limited space, Waldemar gave up his bed and room for Heidi. And they set up a bed in his work area, for him to sleep on until they were able to add another room to the 'Häusle!' Looking back at her last few years in the Sudetenland Erika had always known, it all had to get better in God's time. It had been difficult at times, but Erika robust and stubborn, she had stuck it out, and she had survived. Now 17 years later, Heidi arrived with just one small suitcase. Wearing a simple plain dress, Aunt Heidi, looked old, a little lost she was too, yet all that didn't matter. Crying, hugging and kissing her, Erika was jubilant she had her sister back. Heidi was tallish, a head taller than Erika. She was plump but not fat. Heidi's round face had dark, tired looking eyes. Her hair was snow-white, shoulder length. She looked happy one minute and worried the next.

Stirred by tingling emotions, and the effects of growing excitement, Sepp listened as Erika and Aunt Heidi shared stories and cried together. They did cry a lot. As Sepp witnessed what Heidi went through, he got a better picture about the days and months after WW II ended, and the part of the country he had never seen, his parents' Heimat. At some point, Heidi asked Erika about Frieda, who was born while Erika was alone on the Bauer farm. Here a 'snoopy'

Sepp heard more crying as Erika told Heidi: “Frieda is my child, never mind the father, who may have been Czech, Pole, Russian or whatever. I have no idea which one of those many men it was, and I don’t want to know. Frieda is my daughter, and that's all that counts. Basta!" When Heidi asked her, “So, what about Waldemar, your husband?” Erika admitted: "Waldemar doesn't care much for Frieda. He never did." She added “Maybe it was because I told Waldemar that I have no idea who the father was. Truthfully I admitted to him that it had happened while I was alone on the farm, and many men took advantage of me!”

Aunt Heidi asked about Sepp, "The boy has green-brown eyes, yours are brown where is the green coming from?" Erika's answer was: “That must be from the grandparents!” But as she said what she said, some memories came back. Erika just couldn’t forget the young man, the one with the green eyes, at the station. She knew she would never forget the day she was violated by several men, but it was him who was so different, so gentle, caring and it was him, who helped her to get to the train to the West. “Was he...?" She put the thought aside just like she had done many times before.

Then Heidi talked about: "It was meant to be, that I had my miscarriage. Afterward, I never got pregnant again. Otherwise, the way I emptied out those boys, I would have more children than anyone I know!" And here Erika interrupted and reminded her, that it wasn't a miscarriage, but Heidi had had an unsafe abortion, done by some witch after Heidi came back from White Russia. Erika reminded Heidi: "Your abortion was long before the Nazis came to the Sudetenland. It was after you had dropped that sweet, good-looking Czech boyfriend. Remember you fell for the rebel kid? Your abortion was after you had run away with the crazy Bolshevik teacher, with Igor!" Heidi did not remember him because she asked: "With whom? When?" Erika filled in the gaps by trying to jog her memory: "Heidi remember! You left home and traveled along with your Igor. Then you lived with your Igor for a couple of years in White Russia. That's where you learned to be fluent in Russian!" Heidi still had no recollection what-so-ever. So Erika added: "It was after Igor had died! Remember you told us that Igor got killed in a fight?" Heidi was nodding her head and listening. Erika was trying to jog her memory "Heidi, but you said after Igor was murdered those who had killed him, then got you pregnant. That's why you came back home and looked for a way to get rid of the unwanted child. Remember, you went to the Gipsy woman over there in Friederichsdorf, back home in Sudetenland, who then performed the abortion!" Erika talked to Heidi in great detail about having had a late abortion, being so sick for a month at least and bleeding for weeks after. A dismayed Sepp, who had been eavesdropping, felt like getting sick because he visualized what his aunt Heidi had to go through back then.

The next day in the evening, Sepp listened in as Heidi and Erika were sitting in the kitchen with the oil lamp providing some light. Sepp was next door in the room with the three beds. Heidi talked about her time away from the family farm: "Those American and British men, those were so much nicer than the Czechs and the Poles. They all were just boys, who did it all the same. I wasn't so stupid to refuse any of them but always indicated my willingness to perform as asked. That's what kept me alive!" Then Heidi talked about being with some Russians: "The day after being dragged away from the farm, those Polish guys traded all the meat they had stolen from the farm and my body for fuel because their truck had run out of gasoline." Sepp heard Heidi laughing as she reported: "Those Rusky boys they fed me well! We were drinking and dancing together! We all had fun. These boys were a lively bunch and entertaining."

After a long pause, like being in deep thoughts, Heidi also recalled: "Over the border, in Austria, the American boys all used rubbers, which those others never did." Heidi added: "I was making my way back home, those Slovak boys I was with, they went passed the Sudetenland and over the border into Polish Silesia." Here Heidi revealed what she thought were her worst years in life. Heidi talked about being detained and held prisoner, when trying to find a way back to get over the mountains and home into Sudetenland. "There in Poland, men in Russian uniforms, rounded up females, as they found them in the streets, fields, and living in the woods, and between the bombed out buildings. Those women were all brought to a ‘collection center,’ housed in a former school and gymnasium building. I got picked up when looking for my ride home. After a night at the ‘collection center,’ a group of soldiers marched us all to the train station.” Heidi carried on: “There must have been more than a few hundred women and girls too. Those women were of all nationalities. Many of them were Polish or German speaking. Some talked about being from Scandinavia, to be Roma, to be Slav or Jewish, here and there a voice claimed to be freed from the Nazi camps and having no place to go."

Heidi further described the episode as: "At the train station in the large open area between a waiting locomotive with many wagons designed to carry livestock, and the railway station buildings, soldiers lined us up, in five long rows. We were ordered to undress. Those slowly responding got to feel the soldiers' rifle butts. I noticed one woman who refused to get undressed. She was being kicked by soldiers' boots to the ground, before being dragged away. The rest of us complied when we were ordered to put our clothing in an orderly heap between our feet. Those trying to convince the soldiers that they were Gipsy, Jewish or Scandinavian were silenced fast. One tall skinny older woman had pointed at a tattooed number on her arm and claimed to be Jewish freed from a Nazi camp. She was executed by a pistol shot to her forehead. At the question of 'Who next doesn't belong here?' None of us women dared to raise a voice or hand. It was mid-morning, the warm summer sun made the wait for further orders somewhat bearable. We all were scared. We stood there what felt like a long time, naked, legs slightly spread, guarded by Russian soldiers. Two teams of each four Russian soldiers then walked down the lines four men in front and four behind of us. Those men decided as to what use they had for each of us. Looking at the inspectors approaching, I heard the noise of arriving military trucks, but didn't see anyone!"

In a real serious tone, Heidi carried on: "I knew the train's destination was Siberia. I knew because I had listened to the soldiers talking about having orders for another trainload of healthy women for Siberia. From what I understood that wasn't the first trainload of women, and wouldn't be the last one. I also overheard some fellow in charge pointing out that it was an excellent idea to gather up female laborers instead of males because females work and don't fight, they are easier to break in and more fun to abuse. To them it all made sense."

Heidi explained further: "All elderly, sick and weak looking women were asked to step back and were being led away to an open area next to where dozens of military vehicles were parked. Here they were allowed to get dressed. Those women then were asked to climb on the waiting trucks." Sepp's aunt sounded sad as she continued: "Others like all those young girls, six or eight of them, not even fourteen, and another just about a dozen juvenile females, all younger than eighteen, were asked to pick up their clothing. They were ordered to step forward, to form a line, before being marched to one of the nearby large storehouses for a closer examination. One young girl, with long red hair, started to put her clothing back on. Two soldiers grabbed her. One hit her face, the other took her clothing away, telling her to follow the others and get her ass in the building!" "And that's what was so shocking!" Heidi pointed out: "These were fresh and young girls, adolescent, too young to do hard labor. I watched the last girl entering the train depot storage building. As soon as all girls had disappeared from our view, on the sign of a whistle-blow a large number of young men in Russian uniform who had before been out of sight ran to the very same building, it looked like a race where each of them wanted to get there first."

With a sad, serious voice, Heidi carried on: "We could hear men shouting, then the voices of those girls. Roaring screams were echoing between the buildings. We all knew what was happening! Then the girl with the long red hair came dashing out of the structure. Two men followed. A soldier coming the other way, from the latrine, didn't let the naked girl get away. He stepped in her way and tripped her. Both men who had been chasing her caught up. The two uniformed soldiers grabbed her arms and picked her up. They held her in a firm grip, one on each side. Another man holding his pants up with just one hand real slowly walked over to the trio and slapped her face several times. She made sad weeping noises. He hit her again and again until long animated sounds followed. Visibly turned on by her crying loudly he grabbed her legs, dropped his pants and brutally raped the sobbing and yowling child in front of the soldier who had stopped the girl from running away. Only after he let go of her legs, to pull his trousers up, did he acknowledge the soldier who stood there. After a few words exchanged between both men, with a most generous gesture, the one who had just raped the girl offered the soldier to take his place. Once the latter as well had satiated his titillation with the kicking redhead girl, those other two soldiers, who had been holding her in midair, dragged the squealing and howling girl back to and inside the storage building."

Aunt Heidi kept on talking: "One of the Russians, who acted like he was in charge of the situation, standing near me had gotten rather excited viewing the brutal assault on the innocent young girl. He had noticed me watching him from the corners of my eyes, as he was scratching his balls. That soldier ordered me 'Davai, Frau komm schon!' And I picked up my clothes, and he took me to the train. I got to visit the wagon reserved and used by the guards. By the time he was done with me, the rest of the women, all inspected and found to be able and fit for Siberia, were asked to grab their clothing and were herded onto the cattle wagons. I finally could get dressed too. However, it wasn't long after that I had to take my clothes off again." After a pause, Heidi added: "Yes I got to ride in the wagon used by the soldiers. They even had a wood burning stove for cold nights. After about two hours the train stopped in another town, and another hundred or more women got added to the transport. Then the train didn't stop again until the next day. From here on, at several train stops, some women were being selected and ordered off the train. They were loaded on waiting trucks and hauled away. It was a long ride. I didn't get much sleep. But I got food and stayed warm during the nights. To Siberia, it was a three-day train ride, and there was little food. Many women got sick."

A week later, it was just getting dark. Sepp was finishing his homework, as Erika came home. Then after supper, Heidi was answering Erika's question: "Russia, Siberia, isn't it a most horrible place? What a miracle you survived in such a cold and unfriendly environment!"

"You must know, I was lucky, I always loved men! And I was the only one speaking and writing fluent German and Russian, as well as Czech. While others did slave labor, heavy work, and many died, I was playing good company with the guards and acted as translator as needed." Heidi said with a smile. Then with a sad and very troubled voice, Heidi said: "Erika you will not believe it what I saw. Some of those Russian men they were binge drinkers and drunk unable to perform as men are somewhat expected to; some turned into real wild animals, brute beasts, you wouldn't want to know what they were doing to some of those poor women's bodies!" At that point, Erika vividly remembered what she had witnessed at Ralf Bartsch's farm, and yes she clearly could imagine what men are capable doing to women. Then Heidi stated as a matter fact. "Erika, I lost my mind, I spent too many years in Siberia. It felt like never-ending!" The last place she remembered was called Number 517, Petrozavodsk in Karelia. Heidi said: "I thought I saw Olga our younger sister there too. When I tried to catch up with her, soldiers stopped me. I am not sure, but when I had shouted Olga's name, the same did turn around. She looked skinny and sick. I am entirely certain it was our little sister!"

And Sepp listened to them both sobbing; they were crying!

Another night as Erika and Heidi were sitting in the kitchen and Heidi asked Erika: “What were those Czechs like, the people who stole our farm?” “They were God loving people who had lost their property and much of their family in 1939 to the Nazis. They did accept Frieda and me, and they protected us till we had to leave!” Erika answered. Heidi wanted to know: “When you had to leave home, how did you get to the American Zone in West Germany, instead of Austria or Russia?” “We marched in the snow to the train station, and here a nice young man wearing a brand-new uniform saved my life and got Frieda and me on the train to the West!” Erika said. Heidi’s question of “How did you meet Waldemar?” Got Erika’s “I needed shoes, and that’s how we met!”

Heidi asked Erika: “I know you had been with very few men in your life, until those Russian soldiers. I still can see your face staring at the ceiling. They had undressed us. You were naked on father’s bed, and I was next to you on mother’s bed. I watched those young men, one after the other coming out of the bathtubs and like trying on a new pair of new shoes they got to and in you, one man at a time, before getting out and off and coming to see me. And you didn't scream or fight. Tell me something, as that wasn't what we call having or enjoying a sexual relationship! But aside from letting it happen, did you ever get the kind of special feelings while a man penetrated you, the wanting more of the same, wishing he stayed with you, do everything until he satisfied you?" Erika answered: "Remember you told me that we are just a playground for those boys, go let them play, play with them. Don't fight, play, and make em happy. When they are done playing, they will let you go! Yes! That's all I did, and it saved my life." Then Erika was thinking back at the moment of her first and only orgasms, and it was with that green-eyed young, good looking and so gentle but firm soldier lover. She was going to confess, to tell Heidi about him, but not now, maybe later!

Heidi carried on with: "I asked because I always liked men, I still like men! You must know, in Austria at the hospital. I had that one helper, a young hopper. Bubi sometimes sneaked into my room at night, and other days at daytime. He was new in what we were doing. He had a girlfriend but had never done it with her. She insisted on waiting till the wedding. So I took him under my wings, showed him what I like, and he was getting real good pleasing me, yes, and then I had to leave coming out here to see you. I miss my little Bubi! You know I still like men, never could get too much of them." Heidi added: "Do you remember those Russian soldiers were so happy when they saw the clean underwear and socks I had gathered up for them, you know? They were like kids getting gifts." Erika answered: "I wonder what you would have told our brothers when they returned and had no more clean underwear because you gave them to some Russians to make them feel good?" Both laughed. Heidi ended her story for the night with: "But back in Siberia I just didn't want to die, so I did whatever I could to survive. Best of all I knew what to do, what to say and how to be wanted and needed by the right people. Getting back and to Austria is another story. I am going to tell you all of it at another time. I'm too tired today!"

Aunt Heidi had come to stay with them for good. For good only lasted a short time, until

Erika coming back from field work once at noon found her naked sister in Waldemar's arms. She forgave her once. A week later Erika came home early and again Heidi was with Waldemar in bed. She forgave her twice. A couple of weeks later Erika caught Heidi with Waldemar again. That time, the third time Erika said Heidi must leave. For the sake of peace at home, Erika's sister had to move on. And Heidi's name was never mentioned again.

About the time of Heidi's departure, Waldemar was reading a letter postmarked in Munich. It was to let his father know, that all the missing toys had shown up, and he was sure that Sepp was no thief. The letter was from Karl, Sepp's step-brother.

How little did Karl know? At times while Waldemar was working for another shoemaker in Unterschwarzenberg, Sepp got to ride with his father, as a coworker picked Waldemar up by car. Then, after school, Sepp got to visit with Eddie and play around town until it was time to be driven home. And Sepp was already back then a thief and a liar, he was. One day he took

20DM from the cash drawer at the shoe repair shop, another time he stole money out of his father's wallet too. Yes, young Sepp was a thief. As an avid reader, Sepp had read all the Karl May books by age 12 and had been reading paperbacks, most of them about the 'Wild West' many stolen from Meyer's bookstore at the Stadt-Wall. Sepp had no money but an appetite like an elephant when it came to reading about people and the world and those adventures, which came with it. If there was a place Sepp always wanted to see then it was the Wild West, he wanted to be there, live there and experience the same.

In his dreams, he was there, and as well on days when storming up the rolling hills, running along the river, the bow in hand, while shooting arrows tipped with old sewing machine needles from his father's Singer Sewing machine at random targets.

Sepp looked forward to the summer camps. Here he was allowed to interact with other kids. He was able to prove to himself how competitive he was. Sepp learned chess, and within two weeks he was hard to beat. Sepp went up trees nobody else dared to climb and fell out of some of them, but as he had learned to land on all four, like a cat, he never got hurt aside some scratches and minor cuts, while landing on hands and feet and rolling over as needed.

On rainy days the kids got to play indoors or do fun things like learning needlepoint, to knit, or just learn how-to-use-needle-and-cotton. He heard boys calling it 'girls stuff' not so Sepp. He was quite good with needle and cotton because his father had taught him. Therefore it was understandable that he liked to try his luck with knitting as well, and such he did.

At those summer camps, they had plenty of food, many food items he had never seen and had never tasted before. Even more important for Sepp, here he got to shower with hot water every day. At home, they had no shower. They bathed once a week this was on Saturdays. Water from the well, hand pumped, was heated on the stove, and they all shared it after being poured into a large metal bathtub. Naturally at times, because it was two, three, four, five or six days since the last bath, Sepp smelled. Some well-meaning kids had told Sepp that he stank. But it was just that every day he rode his bike for many kilometers and he did sweat. People perspired, so did Sepp.

The latest summer camp was in the Alps. Sepp with a group of 40 other kids stayed at a Youth Hostel just below an old, very old castle. On their fourth day, they got to visit the same. First the girls, then the boys walked up the hill, arriving at the drawbridge short on breath. Then all met in the castle's courtyard. They got to see the Knights Hall and climbed up-and-down the spiral stairs in the towers. They visited the ballroom. Last, not least they were let down into the torture chamber. Sepp had read about those windowless, soundproof underground rooms where crime and criminal justice was being dealt with by professional torture-masters. Here Sepp got to see an Iron Maiden, and he got a good look at a stretcher, called the Strappado, a simple pulley system. There were also on display: Screws, drills, hammers and pliers and chains and ropes, and hooks, and a fireplace not just for heat, and a variety of large kettles.

That night Sepp did have a nightmarish dream about the Iron Maiden. He couldn't see how it ever had functioned as a torture tool. Closing the hinged cabinet, created in a women's shape, just a wee bit, because of those long sharp spikes on the front and the back, must have been immediate execution. Closing it all the way would only tenderize the meat in-between. Sepp asked Heinrich, one of the young men leading the group activities the next morning: "Ja! Herr Heinrich, please tell me how did they get the Iron Maiden to work, the one with the long thorns, the one we saw at the Schloss (castle)?" And Heinrich their guide and teacher laughed, "Those were mainly used as deterrents, as well as a tool to make people talk. Anyone who was offered either to admit guilt and spill his guts, or to visit the Iron Maiden, would more likely than not, have taken the first option. Sepp, splendid question, but if anyone ever ended up in the spiked mold, it was surely the end for him."

The kids had lots of outdoor activities, which included hide and seek in the park-like wooded settings. They also did nature walks where those who didn't know the native plants got a chance to familiarize themselves with the local flowers, shrubs, bushes, trees, and grasses and weeds. At one of those walks, they watched a mother fox carrying a rodent in her mouth, most likely home to her den to feed the little ones.

Aside from those summer camps, where he was part of a bunch of boys and girls, Sepp was a loner. On school days Sepp left Kleinerort by himself, early in the morning on his bicycle. He rode those 15 kilometers to school in Unterschwarzenberg on the shorter but the hilly route. After school, he bicycled back 18 kilometers, on the easy mainly flat route. After dark, the dynamo on his bike put out enough electricity for the headlight. On cloudy nights with the light turned on, he could see the way. Sepp liked the moonlit nights better because he could see the road in front of him without having to rely on the headlight.

Yes, by now Sepp was old enough to earn his keep, and he knew it was time to replace play-time with actual work. Therefore Sepp did come along when Erika asked him, to a nearby vineyard. Here Sepp helped with the grape harvest, starting at sunrise and climbing up-and-down the hillside all day? The same noble family, who owned the Neuhof, had several vineyards. During harvest time in the fall, as well as trimming vines in early spring, they hired helpers from the surrounding villages. They provided transportation for their workers, to work and after work back home. The pay was excellent and the more hands, the faster the job got done. All those vineyards were on steep slopes impassable to vehicles. According to Erika only goats or physically nimble people could handle the kind of terrain.

Sepp had no school that week. It was the day of the first frost. Grapes for a special late-harvest needed to be harvested within 48hours. Just before dawn, a bus was picking up the workers, and yes Sepp was going to help because Erika had asked him. By sunrise, they were at the vineyard below the castle. They started at the castle walls and worked their way down filling the grape picking baskets on their backs with those frozen full-ripe grapes. At the bottom, they emptied their baskets into big half-barrels on the bed of a field trailer. And they climbed back up with the empty basket on their backs and on the way down they picked those over-ripe partially frozen grapes and threw them into the basket on their backs.

At some time by mid-morning, because it was freezing cold, and the glove covered hands had become stiff, one of the overseers went around pouring shots of distilled wine for everyone, and Sepp liked the feeling. Instantly his body warmed up. His hands were no longer hurting. It was a pleasant feeling. By about ten, they all had sandwiches, at noon they had each a bowl of hot meaty soup, Erika explained that it was ‘Eintopf’ and then sandwiches again in the mid afternoon. They stopped when it got too dark. The bus dropped each one of the workers off at home. Kleinerort was the last stop. Here seven people got off the bus. That night Sepp slept well. The next morning Sepp had a hard time to get up, he who thought to be in excellent shape, had sore muscles. As Erika kept on insisting that he got up, he finally did. They just made it in time to get to their waiting bus. Sepp was looking forward to his glass of wine spirits in the morning. Thanks to having had enough hands they finished by noon. As the bus dropped them off it started to snow, Erika was telling Sepp something about ice-wine, he didn't understand. After getting home, Erika gave him two sugar cubes with Melissengeist because he was complaining about aching all over.

The pay was good, and the experience was an interesting one too. For Sepp it had been hard work, for Erika, it had been just what she did every day, help farmers with planting, weeding, and harvesting.

When it came time to trim the vines back, Erika was going to help to prune the vines at the same vineyard. They did ask her to bring her boy along, and Sepp agreed, a little pocket money couldn't hurt. Again they got a ride to the vineyard, and again they started at the top and worked their way down, it was with pruning shears. It was tedious non-stop look, find the right spot, cut, next look again, and find the right place to cut. All the old dead growth had to go, and the cut back had to conform to the shape of the trellis. That time Sepp lasted only three days, while Erika worked six days trimming vines in the vineyards around the castle.

This spring Sepp had a crush on that one girl. Her name was Lydia. He was 13 years old, and Lydia was 17. She was the one who taught him how to masturbate. Well, it all started out with Sepp taking some army rations to Eddie, his friend in Unterschwarzenberg. He was unable to locate Eddie, so he went down to the lake. That's where he met Lydia. She had a nice 10-speed bicycle and a flat tire. He had a tire repair kit, and she got to watch him take the front wheel off, and removing the tire and the tube. He pumped the tube full with air, put it in water and marked the holes, and there were two. Then he cleaned and sanded the same. He added glue and two patches, and after giving it enough time to dry, he put it all back together, pumped it up and she was ready to go. Sepp had done such a few times before. It was easy for him.

Lydia’s stomach growled while she watched him repairing the flat tire. She admitted being hungry. Attracted to Lydia on first sight, Sepp sacrificed Eddie’s rations, and he fed her some crackers, opened a small can of American cheese, and another small can with chocolate. Lydia was impressed. Lydia was visiting her uncle in Zweiersheim, which was on the way to

Kleinerort, and Sepp accompanied Lydia to her uncle's place. Then he went on his way home. From here on every time Sepp drove by Zweiersheim, he looked for her.

About a week later on a Saturday, on his way to see Eddie, it was Sepp's luck that he watched her on her bicycle coming his way near Unterschwarzenberg. They talked, and at the spur of a moment, Sepp decided to show Lydia one of his favorite scenic spots just beneath the remnants of an old castle tower. It was a warm, humid early afternoon, no clouds in sight. They parked their bikes at one of the birch trees at the bottom of the castle hill. Then they both started out to climb the steep hillside. At times they had to help each other over boulders, and over fallen trees. Sepp just like Lydia was out of breath by the time they reached the top. Here Sepp showed her the paths around the tower and then led Lydia to a place overlooking the valley on both sides and a truly breathtaking scenery. Hidden away between hazelnut bushes Lydia admired the spectacular view down onto the valley below and beyond.

Three people on horseback were crossing the shallow river in the valley, they at least 2 kilometers away. Lydia told Sepp: “My uncle has horses too, he breeds them for jumping and races!” and she asked him: “You know horses need their ‘sheath’ cleaned every so often?” He answered: “Ja! What kind of ‘sheath?” Lydia explained, “That’s the penis!” Seeing an astonished look on Sepp’s face, Lydia laughing at him said: “It’s just like men, they need it too!” “Ja? What? You are lying?” as he had never heard of such a thing.

She noticed that she had aroused Sepp's interest when he asked, "Ja? Really? How?" To satisfy his curiosity, she offered "You want me to show you!" and he did not fight her as she unbuttoned the drop front of his lederhosen. She found and squeezed his penis. She checked and cleaned underneath his foreskin. Then she moved her fingers around and up and down like she was going to milk him. Sepp was getting stimulated, roused to action. There were too many sensations. Aside from being encouraged by her touch, there were feelings he had never felt before, and with an explosion of pain and pleasure came relief of the pressure built up by her actions.

She laughed and then whispered in his ear: "I know. You haven't done it before!" As she kissed him, Sepp didn't know what to do. Soon after, they left, and he accompanied Lydia to her uncle's place before heading back home. One more time they got together a week later, that time she watched him masturbate, while her hand was playing with herself. The sad part was that she was leaving the very next day and going back to her parents' home in Obernbach 30km north of Kleinerort. As they parted ways, Lydia did ask him however: "You are 14 or 15 aren't you?" When he answered "Thirteen, but shall be fourteen next year in January!" he watched her shaking her head, but she said nothing. Lydia had changed his life. The same month he visited her in Obernbach on his bicycle, and it was a full day trip. But Lydia was too busy to see him. She had no more time for him. Yes, she did say, "No Sepp! Please don't come back! My parents don't like it if I see anyone younger than 14. And my boyfriend surely doesn't like it if you come by and visit! And my big brother may give you a spanking!" With an unhappy face and feeling let down by Lydia, Sepp pedaled back home, feeling sorry for himself, as once more what he thought was the beginning of a lasting friendship, was no longer.

Still, he would never forget Lydia. She was the first girl to kiss him on the mouth in a certain way. She also was the first one to tell him: "You have the most alluring green-brown eyes." He didn't dare to go back to Obernbach, but he sent her love-letters, yet she didn't answer any of them. After Lydia his desires of adventure, world travel by land and sea became secondary. Thoughts of a sexual nature opened up a brand new perspective as to what he wanted. When masturbating, he liked the feeling. He wanted to do as he had heard and read about, wanted to have sex. Sitting in the outhouse, Sepp did think about what he had heard, seen, learned so far about those two sexes, the boys and girls. And yes, Sepp had heard and seen guys getting in fights about wanting to be with a girl. Yes, he once watched men hitting each other, with the legs of chairs, while the grocery store girl, walked home by herself from a Gasthaus dance. He was told it was all about her! Sepp liked Luise. She was always friendly to him. Sepp didn't understand. Why were they so possessive? Couldn't she be a friend with more than one guy?

Sepp had learned in class several languages. More correct he had learned in school a lot of vocabularies, Latin, English, and French. During the days when he was riding his bike searching out areas where the American soldiers had their exercises, he was able to use some of his English words, and yes after they had seen him coming and looking around several days in a row, the one or the other soldier talked with him. Sepp's "How do you do!" generally got him a "Howdy!" or a "Hello!" And after he had met the same men several times he got to remember their names. Two of them seemed to be always together. Thus two were Al and Ben. When Sepp introduced himself as Sepp Schuster, Al said: "The Sepp name is the short form of Joseph. Therefore to us 'a Sepp is a Joe.'" His friend Ben agreed. Sepp didn't mind that they called him Joe.

On one occasion they gave him money and asked him to get them beer from the Gasthaus, and he did, he bought a case of beer, strapped it on the back of his bike and brought it out to them. He didn't understand that they each wanted just a bottle of beer. Maybe they didn't realize the high value of their dollars at the local brewery. When he returned the change from the purchase, they laughed and asked him to keep it. And yes they were going to give the bottles and the crate back. Glass and wooden box was not only returnable but being washed and reused. As Sepp was leaving, Al handed him a carton of cigarettes and a box of chewing gum to take home. While giving him those treasures, laughing Al said: "Joe! Say, what about some Fräuleins?"

Back in Kleinerort, Sepp bragged that he had met some Ami soldiers while looking for treasures and aside other items had received a whole carton of Pall Mall cigarettes and a box of chewing gum. Sepp talked much about them, his American friends. Having a carton of cigarettes, suddenly he became the center of interest and admiration in the village. It lasted as long as he handed out cigarettes and chewing gum.

Then there was Fräulein Luise. Her parents owned the only grocery store in Kleinerort. She had just turned 21. At village dances, several fights had been breaking out, all because of who was first going to dance with her, with Luise? As far as Sepp could imagine at the time, that must have been the only reason. Luise was of medium height, neither thin nor plump, with a beautiful round face, big blue-green eyes, and straight long blond hair. Every time Sepp bought something at her store, and Luise was helping him; she gave him a big smile and one candy. She was nice. He liked her a lot. Sepp also had been very uncomfortable when listening to her father bawling her out, loud enough that half the village could hear it. Sepp did see her crying, sitting in the corner of the store, once too. That was after her father had been angry with her and told her and the world: "You can't do anything right. Picking up men, like that guy from Hinterberg, a no good prick from a Catholic family, they don't even have a pot to piss in, and that's the guy you pick for a date. Your choices in men are getting worse every day! You never find a good one to marry you, aren't you ashamed of yourself?"

It was Luise who came to Sepp and was telling him: "I always wanted to meet one of these Amis. I promise you anything just say it, if I have it, I give it to you. Could you please-please introduce me to your American friends." Luise looked like she meant it and her "...bitte sei so gut!" was ringing in his ears. Sepp was aware of Ben and Al looking for Fräuleins, so over eagerly he told her: "Ja! I am going to tell Al and Ben what you said." And she hugged him and whispered "...danke schoen!" in his ear.

The next day Sepp was looking all over the place for Ben and Al. Finally, he found their group, doing their exercises. Al saw Sepp, "Joe what's up?" And Sepp was telling him about Luise from the Kaufmann grocery store. As Ben joined them, Al was filling him in: "Joe thinks he knows one Fräulein who wants to date!" "Yes Joe, you have one Fräulein, for Al or me?" And Sepp didn't know what he was talking about therefore not knowing any better said "Ja! Al and you, both, Luise is a strong German Fräulein!" And both Al and Ben were smiling. Ben said "Okay Joe!" Both were off duty three days later on a Saturday, so they made plans. Ben suggested, "Let's all go to see a movie?"

“There is a movie theater in Unterschwarzenberg!” Sepp let them know. Al agreed, “Movie sounds good!” Ben proposed: “On Saturday we come here and pick Joe up first. He then introduces us to his Fräulein Luise, and all together we drive to the movies in Unterschwarzenberg.” Seeing Sepp’s face and the question mark on it hearing his: “Ja! How do I get home, without my bike?” And Al promised: “Yes and after the movies, we are going to take you home. After that, we give Luise a ride to her place too!” “Ja! I am on my way to tell her!” Sepp said and left toward Kleinerort.

All ecstatic, Sepp was in a great hurry to bring Luise the good news. He found her in the store. But she didn’t want him to talk about the Amis in the store because someone may listen. He had to come back after the store closed, and he did. Luise was sweeping the street in front of the store, which was swept already and clean, but she kept on polishing the cobblestone with her broom until Sepp showed up. He overwhelmed her with his news: “Fräulein Luise my two Ami-friends Al and Ben are going to pick me up at noon to go to the movies in Unterschwarzenberg. They want to meet you.

Can you come with us on Saturday?" Luise's face was lighting up, and she was not only accepting the invite but was jubilant overflowing with joy singing: "Sepp did it, Sepp did it!" and getting more serious she told him "Jawohl, this weekend, on Saturday, ausgezeichnet! Ja doch! My parents are both going to visit my aunt in Nuremberg all weekend. What am I going to wear? Where do you want us to meet? Not here at the store! How about at the big old chestnut tree? Near the river!" Sepp confirmed, "Luise we shall pick you up on Saturday at noon at the old chestnut tree on the other side of the village!"

Sepp went right back to search for and find Ben and Al. They were waiting for him to come back with Fräulein Luise's answer. Sepp talked to Ben, who sounded very pleased: "Joe we appreciate your effort, I know Al is already all excited about the Fräulein." Ben added "Listen, Joe, I am looking forward to Saturday, we shall pick you up first. We know where you live, up there outside the village at the shoemaker place. See you at 12noon Saturday! Here is something for you." Another carton of cigarettes changed hands, Pall Mall it said on the box. Sepp was in seventh heaven and getting home he gave the carton of Pall Mall to Waldemar, who thanked Sepp and told him: “Don’t forget to thank your American friends! Those American Cigarettes are valuable, high priced barter goods.”

On Saturday Ben and Al were punctual. All stirred up emotionally, Sepp stood outside the shoemaker shop. He had never before been to a movie, this now was going to be the opportunity, and best of all he was going with his friends and Fräulein Luise. Sepp wore his favorite knee length lederhosen. Awaiting the arrival of his American friends, he saw them coming up the street. It was a big American station wagon. Ben was driving. Sepp got in the backseat. Heading towards Kleinerort, Al asked him: “Joe, what about Fräulein Luise?” Before Sepp could answer, they saw her. Ben’s “Look, Al, how pretty, our Fräulein Luise! How stimulating?” had Al smiling all over his face as he said, “Yes! Isn’t she a turn on?”

Luise Kaufmann was waiting patiently under the big old chestnut tree outside Kleinerort. She was wearing her Sunday church dress. On the way to the movies, Sepp and Luise were sitting in the back of the large American car. Luise was elated and obviously nervous. Sepp could tell as he watched her twisting her hands and fingers. She also moved restlessly in her seat, at one time she was holding Sepp's hand. They all arrived at the movie theater somewhat early. It was not even 1 o'clock in the afternoon, and the movie theater wasn't opening until 6 in the evening. Al pointed at the Gasthaus Zum Storch across the street from the movie theater. Ben agreed, and Luise followed them. The last one to catch up with them was Sepp who had his eyes glued on the film preview and advertisement displays. Sepp knew about the movie theater, and he was looking forward seeing the motion picture. At the Gasthaus Zum Storch, the grown-ups had a few beers and schnapps, and a 'Radlermass' being beer watered down with sparkling water, for Sepp. After the second shot of schnapps, Luise was no longer shy. Three or was it four shots of schnapps and two beers loosened her up. After going to the bathroom on return, Sepp got to watch a happy easy-going Luise. Her eyes were bright and shiny. Her talk and actions were unworried. Luise was enjoying herself. He heard Luise asking Ben: "We go someplace? You and me?" And Sepp watched her foot rubbing Ben's leg. Spirited and relaxed Luise was leaving the Gasthaus on Ben's arm.

Al asked: "Joe what you think, should we head up into the hills and visit the forests?" "Ja! Excellent idea!" Sepp said, knowing that from the hill past the castle the view down at Unterschwarzenberg and the valley beyond was impressive. It was a beautiful day, not too warm, a mixture of clouds and blue sky, a gentle wind, a great day to go for a walk. To pass the time, they went for a ride in the big American Rambler car. Sepp was now sitting up front with Al, the driver, while Ben shared the backseat with Luise. Those two on the wide backbench were quite lively. Sepp heard Ben trying to speak German using words like "Liebe Dich" and Luise answering "Ja good, you good, me right happy!" using her limited English vocabulary. Sepp overheard Luise's "You kiss good! You liebe mich! You do mach love mit mir?" Apparently, they were enjoying each other's company. Sepp tuned into the sounds from the backseat listened to heavy breathing followed by an "Oh sweet!" followed by a "Gut mach schon hin...! Keep on! Magste das schon leiden? Do you like it? ...ohhhh! Oooooh ja!"

Al drove very slowly up the hill past the castle, he found a forest road and followed it into the woods, here he stopped and lit up a cigarette. Al with a smirky smile said to Sepp: "Joe don't watch, you may be too young for that or what?" Sepp didn’t know what to say, but it made him want to see what he wasn't supposed to witness. Sepp got to see Ben between Luise’s legs and doing some humping and pumping, as she was breathing loud, and doing some “Ohhhjaaaaaa, Ahhhhjjaaa, Ohhhjaaaaaa.” Then Ben slowed down. He did one, two, three more pushes, and stopped. Asking Al for a cigarette, Ben climbed off Luise. She hastily covered her wet, curly-bushy medium blonde hair, while smiling at Sepp. He smiled back. In high spirits, playful Luise threw him a kiss. Then she was blushing. Her eyes were glowing. Luise somewhat drunk and high on love looked triumphal. Ben switched seats with Al. As Ben got into the driver seat, Sepp watched Al undoing his pants, and a laid-back Luise was expecting him. She spread her legs wide. With keen interest Sepp watched Luise’s hand lifting her skirt and rubbing her curly hair and in-between her legs. “Ja! Just like Lydia did when she watched me masturbating!” Sepp thought while watching Luise using her other hand to guide Al, to and into her.“

Sepp didn’t comprehend what Al said! However Luise’s: “Tue so, richtich, tiefer! Tuste doch ganz rein! All the way! Ja gut so! Yes! Oh ja, jaaaaajaaaaaah! Oooohjagoood!” Sepp understood. Now Al did just like Ben had done before, in and out, up and down. Sepp got rather nervous, by watching them, but didn’t want to admit anything. So he looked the other way but kept on eavesdropping. It wasn’t more than ten minutes that Ben finished what he was doing with Luise. He asked Sepp: “Joe, come sit in the back and let our Fräulein Luise squeeze in between us men up front.” They switched places. Some of Luise’s attire was back there too, like the bra, and her undies. Sepp couldn’t see all they did up front. He listened to Luise’s happy, chirpy sounds, and ecstatic laughing and the jovial sounds from Ben, accompanied by Al’s peppy vivacious words of praise and encouragement to keep on doing whatever Luise did. Al stopped the car, up on the hill with a view at Unterschwarzenberg below. Sepp looked at the city. Those three up front on the front-seat-bench were changing positions, now Luise’s rear end was towards Al and her head in Bens lap. Al looked at Sepp and suggested: "Joe why don't you go for a walk and come back when I honk the horn?" And he took some dollar bills out of his shirt pocket and put them in Sepp's hand with a wink of the eye. Sepp didn't need to be asked twice, he understood. Aside from everything else Sepp needed to piss real badly. Finding a tree to water was easy.

After parking in the same spot for maybe half an hour, Al honked the car's horn. Sepp returned, and the first thing he noticed were those steamed up windows and a new to his nose not unpleasant yet different musty, stale smell with a hint of cigarette smoke. Al drove slowly back down to the movie house. He parked in front of the Gasthaus Zum Storch. While Ben and Luise were occupied with getting their clothing rearranged, Al went and bought movie tickets for all.

Sepp asked: "Ja! Fräulein Luise, do you want these!" And he held her undies and bra up in the air. She looked at Ben. He was shaking his head. Luise said: "Ben thinks I don't need em at the movies, just leave em there for later, I better don't forget those, when I get home!" Still, plenty of time for another drink at the Gasthaus Zum Storch, and after a trip to the bathroom, Ben bought drinks for all. That time Sepp got a regular draft beer. He was thirsty and emptied his glass in two gulps. He got his refill. Ten minutes before the movie started, the four of them strolled over to the theater and went to their seats. Here at the movies, Luise sat between Ben and Al. Sepp sat a few rows behind them because that's what Ben had asked him to do. He also had given Sepp 10 one-dollar bills. Sepp was rich now. First the money Al gave him, now Ben's ten bucks. He already knew that he was going to spend it all at Meyer's bookstore. Sepp was watching part of the film, yet was mainly looking at and listening to Luise and her suppressed laughter, the joy, and happiness in her voice. Sepp was rubbing his penis. He masturbated and used the spermatozoon to add a little extra shine to the flap of his lederhosen. Sepp was glad it was dark, and nobody saw him.

Leaving the movie house, before taking Sepp home, the four made another stop at the Gasthaus Zum Storch for one more drink before getting on the road. After more beer, Sepp was all comfortable sitting in the back of the

Rambler. In front, Ben was driving. Luise was spread out across the front seat bench, her head first on Ben's shoulders than in Ben's lap and her legs and rear on Al's side. There was a lot of giggling between little bursts of screams and chuckling noises from Luise. Sepp didn't see any what was going on, up front. These three, they undoubtedly were having a ball. It must have been close to midnight that they dropped Sepp off at home. A worried Erika was still up waiting for him. Yes, Waldemar had told her that he was going to the cinema with his American friends. Still, she was concerned.

Two days later, Luise found Sepp; she asked him not to tell anyone. She made sure he understood: "...nothing had happened anyhow! They both, Al and Ben used French Letters." Yes, she Luise was going to see them soon again. With a big kiss, a long kiss pressed right smack on Sepp's mouth she ran off.

"French Letters?" Sepp asked himself, not knowing what she was talking about, but she was already gone. He could still taste her lips. Those big soft lips had left an impression on him.

And she was gleeful. His American friends were satisfied too, so all those three did was drink and fick and watch a movie. About ficken thus sounded so glamorous, "... ficken and besoffen sein ist des kleinen Mannes Sonnenschein...," he had heard quite often. Surely it must be somehow, somewhat unique, so Sepp thought. Sepp wanted to do some humping too, yeah, yes that's what was lately more often than not on his mind.

Sepp had watched when his mother took one of the goats to get inseminated! That was a day trip. At the right time of the month, and only Erika knew what day, that's when she walked the goat 5 kilometers one-way to Unterheim. Half a day it took through the forests, to the old lady with those male goats, half a day back! Erika had to pay every time for her goat to get humped. That wasn't cheap, but Erika said, "I am better off with female goats, than male ones." She explained "Does, female goats don't fight, and they give milk!" Hadn't he also witnessed their female dog in heat, being humped by every dog from the village? And the rabbits he had watched them doing their business as well. Sepp had eyeballed from a distance a bull inseminating a cow. "Doing it that way, so what is the big deal? Is it just like breeding farm animals? Is that all there is to it?" He wondered.

Neither the goats, their dog, the rabbits or the cow nor the bull, none of them looked much different, before while and after being engaged in the humping process. Luise however as well as All and Ben did look quite turned on before, they did laugh and had fun playing with Luise, who enjoyed being played with and doing it. Then afterward they acted quite sprightly because they had a real good time, looking forward to more, all proud of their performance. And Sepp asked himself: “What’s the dissimilarity?” A light bulb went on in Sepp’s busy mind: “It must have all been because of the libations, the beer, and the schnapps!”

Sepp learned much from reading. He was reading a lot. And there was a time in his life when he felt like Siegfried the Nibelungen hero. With whatever represented Siegfried's sword, he went through the nearest rye field and mowed down the aggressive hordes of attackers. Sepp knew as Siegfried nothing could kill him, except the arrow to the heart from the back. Sepp was a cowboy today and then an Indian chief the next day, collecting scalps. As a cowboy, he hunted those bad Indians, the next day he was a famous gunslinger surviving all shootouts. Sepp next became the Marshall, who shot faster than anyone else, and he then again was dreaming about being the greatest train-robber, in the Wild West's history. It was so easy for Sepp to slip into each of those various personalities and to play their roles, just as he had read about in all those adventure books. But there was so much he didn’t learn from books, he had to experience by himself to be able to play such roles.

Sepp knew how it felt to be alone in a classroom full of kids. After school being all by himself, he was however quite comfortable in his skin. Those other school children in Unterschwarzenberg had young parents. They also had brothers and sisters. They lived in beautiful modern homes with electricity and indoor plumbing. They wore fashionable clothing too. Unhappy, envious some days Sepp surely didn't want what he had, he wanted what they, those others had. One day Sepp made a promise, after reading Faust: "If I ever get riches, electricity, telephone, car, house, money, high position, and a pretty wife, I too gladly let the Devil have my soul!" And next, he was contemplating how he would live his life once he was going to be a very rich man. He dreamed about a castle on an island, and every variety of food there is, an everlasting smorgasbord. However Sepp's thoughts got interrupted, Erika needed him to help her with harvesting potatoes. It was her answer because he had asked her for money to buy a set of new bicycle tires.

Sepp helped with the potato harvest up at the Neuhof farm. As the potato fields were all up in the hills on the sandy plateau, he asked: "Why do you grow your potatoes up here and not in the valley?" Ulrich told him: "The sandy soil is ideal for growing potatoes!" Ulrich was driving his tractor and equipment through the rows digging up the potatoes. Many hands, a dozen helpers including Erika and Sepp were harvesting and bagging the potatoes, nice big potatoes, into potato bags. At some time Ulrich made a little fire, and they all had fresh baked potatoes, and those were good, they truly were different. But then again maybe it was just because Sepp was hungry from working in the fresh air. Again it was tedious work doing the same over and over. It just wasn't what Sepp had in mind as his future. He liked the pay but didn't like the kind of work. It was not for him. He wanted to see the world, meet the wealthy and famous, and he was fascinated by thrills and adventures. Picking up and bagging potatoes was nothing more than a most boring routine, so he thought.

Having bought his new tires, and showing them off, Sepp was upbeat. Then Sepp had some papers for school to be filled in. The number of times when he had asked his mother to fill out papers like these, she always did. When he brought these in, every time, it never failed, the teacher who had requested the information was asking: "Who wrote that?" And when Sepp answered: “My mother,” every time he was confronted with the question: “Can't she write?” Therefore, Sepp was ashamed of his mother not being able to write well. That was not what she did best. Best she did being the very best mother he ever had. That too he didn't understand at the time.

Then one day, Sepp saw Erika cry when she heard that Waldemar had made shoes for one redhead single woman, who had just moved to Kleinerort and was living by herself in the village. People were talking about Waldemar stopping by her place quite often, having lunch there too. In a small village, rumors start fast!

How disappointing for Erika, but she never said it, when she did not see Sepp becoming what she wanted him to be, namely an engineer. By age 13 all Sepp wanted was to get away from the Lutheran Village, from Kleinerort. There was no future for him in the little village with one Gasthaus on the left side of the road, and another on the right side.

Sepp did ride his bicycle all over the place, and he was good on it, he was. Oh ja, he was. On one of his trips on his bike, he saw Ben again. He and his men were in a training exercise not too far from Kleinerort. The word was that Luise was engaged, not to Al or Ben, they were already married, and their wives were waiting for them back in America. But they had introduced Luise to a young single officer, and those two were flying later the same month to America to get married. As Sepp was heading back to Kleinerort, Ben gave him two cartons of cigarettes, and a box of chewing gum. Sepp instantly felt like the richest guy in the world.

Sepp's mind now often was occupied with the thought to get to do it like he had seen Ben and Al doing it with Luise in the Rambler. As Sepp was so shy, it just did not happen for him. He had dreamed about doing it with Luise because she had promised to do anything if he would introduce her to his Ami friends. He had been too afraid to ask her. There also was the girl Eddie knew. Christel was her name. Eddie had introduced her to Sepp. She supposedly was open-minded and not shy when it came to recreational sex. Eddie had said: "You need to give Christel a try, she likes to fick, and the sensual arousement which is part of doing it." Sepp had chickened out. He didn't know how to get started, how to ask, what to say or to do.

Sepp gave one carton of cigarettes to his father. The second carton he gave to Eddie, his friend. Sepp had been racing with Eddie on roller skates in the summer and ice-skating in the winter. They had played ice hockey together too, Eddie was cool. He knew him now for about two years. Eddie had always been a friend. He lived in Unterschwarzenberg two blocks away from Sepp's Oberrealschule. Eddie's father was a truck driver. His mother worked for the railroad company. Sepp had spent several nights at Eddie's place. This year so far twice, during heavy rain and hail, Sepp had an open invitation from both Eddie and his mother to stay at Eddie's place overnight, any time the weather was too bad to ride home to Kleinerort. Eddie was a lively and witty boy, and Sepp would have liked to be more around him. Going to different schools, and being on different schedules, hadn't allowed for more than seeing each other once a week lately. Eddie had plans for Sepp. He wanted Sepp to get it on with Christel, known to Eddie's friends as a playful, and seductive girl. Her girlfriend was supposed to be quite a libidinous amateur too. The gossip about those two girls was that they did men for a living. It was the kind of talk which interested Sepp. Eddie said: "Those girls have been doing it with Ami soldiers for cigarettes and army rations, ever since they had their first period! At least that's what some folks told me!" Also based on hearsay those girls, Christel now 17 and Lottie the 18 years old, were really fun to do. According to the word on the street both were known as trashy and cheap.

The carton of cigarettes in his hands Eddie explained, "Those two girls parents are dead; by bartering what they have, they are doing okay, but more importantly they like doing it! Let's do some ficken tonight. My parents are not home..." so Eddie said. Then asking Sepp: "...you done it already?" Sepp not wanting to admit his innocents was leading Eddie on by answering: "I know all about ficken!" In the back of his mind, he was thinking of how he had watched those rabbits at home, every so often. And yes, he had watched Luise and Al and Ben.

A few days later, coming to find out that that's what Eddie had done with the carton of cigarettes, that he had traded the smokes for sexual favors from those two girls. Sepp now wished he had been there too. It was then while Sepp was getting the inside scoop on Eddie's lighthearted adventures with Christel and Lottie,

Sepp felt bad about having chickened out. Then Eddie also told him about another girl he had a crush on and a sexual adventure with: "Her name was Lydia, she was 17. She was here for one summer only. That Lydia used to ride her bike into Unterschwarzenberg, and we did it in the bushes, near the fence, at the lake, in the back of the park. Lydia was getting all worked by watching me masturbate, while she did the same playing with herself. I got to do so with her several times. Then the last time I wanted to fick her real bad, but she fought me off!" Eddie was shaking his head "Asking her why not! She told me, that first of all we can't do it without French Letters, second I am not ready to go all the way, and third enough of this, I don't want to see you no more!" Eddie explained that he felt being led on by her. Because he was sure, she was doing her foreplay and was waiting for him to make a move. He didn't like to be teased and dropped like she did to him. "I was real pissed at her. I did let the air out of her bike's tire. I hit a nail with a rock, twice in her front-tire. Then I put my skates on and skated up the hill to the castle, just to get away from her and to work it off. By the time I rolled back down into town several hours had passed, and I was kind of okay. I ran into

Christel, in the back of the park at the lake. I told her about my ruined sex-life, about how turned on I was, but no place to go. Christel was so funny. She bent over a park bench, then asked me to do her from behind. Once, noticing I was done, Christel asked me 'feeling better my friend?'" Eddie was looking up to the sky, scratching his butt said: "No! I haven't seen Lydia ever since. She was so stuck up super standard conservative in public places, but under the bushes she let loose. And yes, Sepp I must tell you every time watching Lydia wetting her undies, I got a charge out of it! Yes, she was freakish!" Eddie added: "But Christel, yes she is natural, you need a date with her! What do you think?"

Sepp was listening quietly. He didn't know if he should reveal to Eddie, that he had fixed Lydia's flat tire while looking for his friend. He also wasn't sure if he should disclose to him his very own attempts to date and hanging out with the very same Lydia. Sepp decided to keep his mouth shut and postpone talking about Lydia till a later time.

Sepp was 13, going on 14 and old enough to work. Sepp felt that he knew enough, more than most people in his closest surrounding. Time to use what he knew and earn some money too, time to take care of his own. Sepp also had started a stamp collection when he was five. The stamps were sorted by country only, and most stamps were still on envelopes. Eddie's mother had given Sepp a large box filled with envelopes too. Sepp's stamp collection kept on growing. He was dreaming of hitting the jackpot by finding a rare stamp and getting rich overnight.

Sepp's mother with Waldemar's help had been able to make a down payment on a small house in Windsheim, 20 kilometers from Kleinerort. It was for Frieda, who was pregnant, without a husband. Windsheim was much bigger, had several thousand homes and it also had some industry. Erika drove her moped back and forth, a 40km round trip from Kleinerort to Windsheim. Yes, Erika was determined to do whatever necessary to get Frieda settled down in her very own place.

Waldemar was now 73, still working, repairing shoes. Sepp was old enough to work too, and he knew that it was time to do so. He had done some work in a nearby vineyard. He had helped several times now harvesting grapes starting at sunrise and climbing up-and-down the hillsides all day. He also knew how to trim vines. Sepp had worked once or twice in the fields too. No! He didn't like that kind of work. By now Sepp had only one goal: "Ja! I must earn a living, get on my own feet, get away from home, yes, get far away from Kleinerort!" Sepp was eager to leave home, but he was not ready just to take off and leave without knowing where to sleep and what to eat. Sepp knew most important for him were free housing and free food, second most important getting paid, and third most important he wanted to see the world, the big cities, high society and how the very wealthy people live. Sepp's vision for his future included: "Ja! I can become a steward on the most luxurious Ocean liner, or be a waiter, or be a cook in any of the many luxurious resorts around the world, somewhere near the Ocean." Therefore Sepp went to the "Arbeitsamt" (German Federal Employment Agency) in Unterschwarzenberg and asked for work. The gentleman looked at Sepp. Once he knew what Sepp wanted, like food, place to sleep, in a luxury place, he suggested an apprenticeship at a luxry hotel. And on his first try, Sepp got offered an apprenticeship as a waiter in Altestadt at one of the world's finest Luxury hotels. And yes it included free room and board. He was going to get paid 20DM, the standard monthly amount of pocket money for apprentices at the time. He also was going to meet people of 'Class, Fame and great Wealth.'

After all the necessary papers had been signed and accepted by the employer and Sepp's parents, it was soon time to leave home. Waldemar had a pair of black pants tailored for Sepp, and he made sure Sepp had several pairs of black socks. The day before Sepp left. Waldemar took him to a uniform and work clothing store in Unterschwarzenberg. Here they picked up two white work shirts. These shirts were of good quality and made to last, and they came with detachable collars and cuffs. Both waiters' shirts were extra-long in the back and shorter in the front. His father explained the reason that all good shirts are longer in the back and shorter up front with: "It takes more material to wrap up bacon than it takes to wrap a sausage." With the two shirts Waldemar bought him six collars and six cuffs, those easily attached and by having so many to change out, his father tried to make sure that Sepp would always look prim and proper dressed. The next day in the morning Waldemar handed Sepp a new pair of black work shoes, he had made for him.

Sepp was happy to escape from Kleinerort. He carried his work shoes, socks, and underwear in the rucksack on his back. In his left hand was the suitcase. The one Traude had bought for him at the KaDeWe in Berlin, while the right hand was searching for bus fare in the depth of his pants' pocket. Sepp wore his beloved 'Knickerbocker style lederhosen,' and he was all smiles as he got on the bus to Altestadt.

A lady sitting in the seat in front of Sepp was telling her kids sitting next to her about the Buergermeistertrunk: "Way back when the Swedes were ransacking and burning down every town, they got to Altestadt. They were getting ready to attack the city when the Buergermeister (mayor) rode out from Altestadt on his donkey. And he asked the leader of the Swedes, to save Altestadt. He offered to fight with the commander for the sake of his town. The chief of the Swedes was a tall battle-hardened man, who had never yet lost a match. The Swede looked at the older fellow with the beer-belly and laughing accepted to fight for the preservation of Altestadt. As he was entirely sure that he was going to win, he left the choice of weapons up to the Buergermeister. The mayor chose beer! And they drank a lot, in the end, it was the Buergermeister who won. The Swede keeping his word asked his troops to leave Altestadt alone. That's how it got saved, and that's why we can still enjoy the beauty of the old walled city!"

The bus arrived right on time in Altestadt. Overflowing with anticipation, holding his small suitcase in the right hand, Sepp was the first to step off the blue and white bus at the bus-stop in Altestadt. Here he was, just outside the historic town.

Sepp had arrived in the Medieval Town, in the southern part of Germany. The ancient walled town on the bank of the river Tauber was a relic from another time. Inside the tall and robust stone walls, the use of cars was widely limited. Large trucks and buses were not able to pass through the narrow gate-towers. It was Sepp's first visit to the town, untouched by the wars, unchanged since ancient times. As the lady on the bus had been talking about the upcoming Buergermeistertrunk, Sepp wanted to see it too. Sepp was going to visit and see everything there was to see in the museum-like town. Surely he would get souvenirs for the few people back home, who had envy written all over their faces when he told them about his moving to Altestadt.

The apprenticeship contract for the finest place in town weighted heavily in his suitcase. His dreams had become a reality. Sepp did not have to go back to the Oberrealschule (High school), to the teachers who didn't understand him and his 'Wander's Lust.' He would not have to return to where the Lutheran kids had been laughing at Sepp, him the Catholic child of impoverished war-uprooted Sudeten-German parents. Most of all, he would never again be forced to go to church on Sundays. And he did not have to go to confessions either. Indeed, he would be allowed to have secrets too. Independence and wealth were waiting for Sepp. He hopped from the sidewalk onto the rounded cobblestones, polished by hoofs and wheels, a street traveled since ancient times by peasants and noblemen alike. The stones looked slippery in the sunlight. Sepp skipped over a few of these cobblestones and jumped back onto the pedestrian walkway. Everywhere he looked lovely flower pots, clean streets, and well-kept buildings. Sepp stopped and examined the various flowers in the window boxes. He didn't know the plant names yet the blue, and the white and the yellow flowers were beauteous and plentiful.

Standing in front of one of the fortified wall towers, he admired the city walls all made of solid stone. And above he could see the covered walkway running the length of the wall, around the city. In front of Sepp, rows of houses built in the traditional Franconia style. Brown structural beams exposed to the viewer, acting as a framework, bearing whitewashed mortar, covering the variety of stones used as building material. The gabled roofs were mostly red tile, and here and there an artisan had covered one in black slate. Real antiquities were everywhere for sale, so were look-a-likes. Colorful postcards and trinkets got Sepp's attention for a moment.

The few DMs left in his pocket stayed there. Sepp planned to do his shopping after receiving his first 20DM paycheck.

At the most famous Luxury Hotel, his new workplace, a dressed up older gentleman, opened the door for Sepp only halfway. Sepp found himself caught between door and door-frame. Showing no interest in letting Sepp pass the door-keeper asked: “Young man where are you from? Where do you think you are going?” Sepp opened his suitcase and showed him the apprenticeship contract. That’s when the doorman handed Sepp off to a bellhop with the words: “Take the kid to Frau Holle at H&R.” Young Sepp resented being called a kid. He had no choice but followed the bellboy down the hall, around three corners, and to an elegant office. Here Sepp was greeted by a wealthy-looking rich-dressed lady with spectacles hanging from a gold chain. After checking Sepp’s papers, she stared in a fiercely piercing manner at his pants. Before looking him over from head to foot. Sepp didn’t know why she was giving him those looks. Then she asked: “Sepp! You did bring black pants and a white shirt, did you?” He had noticed her glaring at his shiny oiled and buttered up lederhosen. “Ja! Yes, in my suitcase!” Sepp answered. Now, satisfied with his reply she called for Otto, whom she asked to show Sepp his living quarters. Sepp trotted along following Otto, out the back door of the hotel down the road to a building in a side street. Otto warned him: “Never use the front door again when you go to or leave the hotel. We are to use the servant's entrance, after all, we are servants!” “Ja! Yes, I shall only use the back doors!” Sepp acknowledged the lesson.

Otto was also a waiter’s apprentice. He was at the end of his second year “One more year to go, and I get to make real money, like every waiter, and I shall get my very own apartment and my Danish furniture!” Otto said as they walked down the street. “I don’t like all the old overstuffed and over-decorated furnishing. I want it all plain nice the Scandinavian style, you know?” And Sepp had no idea what Otto meant with Danish and Scandinavian style. They arrived at another impressive looking very-very old building. The paint looked fresh. Otto opened the old wooden entrance door. The squeaking hinges were crying for a sip of oil. As Sepp stepped inside, he realized the old building was only on the outside renovated, inside it was used for storing furniture and whatever. Otto showed Sepp up a wobbly creaking circular staircase to a tiny 'kammer' under the gabled roof. Someone had crammed one bunk and two single beds into a small room. It was warm, the air stuffy. The smell of unwashed socks was lingering in the air. Two very tired-looking lockers, for the shoes and clothing, leaned outside in a short hallway, holding each other up. Compared to where he came from, it was an improvement for Sepp. Otto pointed at the bunk bed: "I sleep on the top!" Otto let him know "You get the lower one!"

Otto had to go back to work, not without telling Sepp: "Feel at home, get comfortable. Toilette and shower are downstairs. You can't miss them! My shift is over by around 7, and I will bring you some food as well, the other two beds belong to Gustav and Walter, they are bellhops, and you shall meet them as they get here."

After stuffing his backpack and suitcase under the bed, Sepp sat on the lower bunk. His stomach was growling. He decided to have a look around and to familiarize himself with his new home. Downstairs behind heaps of small cardboard boxes and several large unopened plywood crates, there was the bathroom, and it was indoor plumbing. Sepp was used to the smell of outdoor facilities, the outhouses at home, the smell was okay. From the looks, the toilette had never been cleaned and had a dark brownish-black layer where one may have expected to see porcelain. There was also a big cast-iron bathtub, with a rusting showerhead above. The bathroom must have been at one time all tiled. Now tiles were missing and broken, the empty squares in-between were covered with grayish, brown and black mildew. It showed that nobody had taken the time to give it a cleaning. Semi-washed underwear was hanging from a washing line strung from one wall to the other. It wasn't so much the dirt. Sepp was jubilant to know there was running water and a shower. It was the musty smell in the air, which he couldn't identify because he had never smelled such before. Walking back to the staircase to his heavenly accommodation, he admired the water spots on the ceiling and areas where loose plaster was hanging on, undecided, not yet ready to fall and visit the bits and pieces of plaster on the floor.

As it was getting late in the day, he met his roommates, the two bellboys, Gustav and Walter. They were nice fellows, working for the same most elegant high rated hotel. None of them sounded happy. Gustav was the one who had shown him the way to H&R earlier. Here now Gustav was saying: “I don’t like her, the owner!” Sepp had not met her yet, based on what Sepp heard, that lady was a tightwad, money-grubber, cheapskate, and frugal to the point that she fed only leftovers to the staff and what they didn’t eat, went all back into the stockpots. At her place, nothing got wasted. Walter said: “She is so money hungry that she has everyone working at least two extra hours each day without pay.” Sepp listened to what his roommates had to say, yet he didn’t mind. He needed a job and a place to stay, and some food, so, all in all, he got what he had asked for.

Then Otto showed up. He brought several bottles of lemonade and a bunch of sandwiches. Sepp had three of the sandwiches; he wolfed them down, never looked at what they had put between the slices of bread because he was so hungry.

On his first day at work, Otto instructed Sepp, by telling and showing him how to clean and polish the silver, the brass, and copper items. Then Otto was called away to help with setting up a banquette room. Running out of the silver cleaner, Sepp asked one of the waiters: "Where can I get more Sidol, the silver cleaner, the Metallpolitur?" Sepp waited and finally went looking for the waiter who had said: "I know where they keep it. I bring you another can of Sidol!" Sepp was walking out of the back of the house into the front of the house. He entered the vestibule, the hallway towards the lobby and the dining areas. Lured by the splendor displayed at the Hotel, the tapestries, the old swords, the dented shields and full body armor, Sepp went to explore his new surroundings. A huge painting in a carved gilded frame caught his eye. It was in much the same style as the paintings he had seen in several old castles and in churches. Paint flakes were peeling off in two corners. However, the work of art was not about saints and angels. It showed men in long robes staring at a beautiful smiling woman on a white horse. No saddle was on the horse's back, not even a blanket. Only long flowing blond hair covered the woman's nudity. Sepp tried to read the engraved brass sign on the carved frame. A group of noisy hotel guests stopped next to him. Sepp looked around in the spacious lobby and felt out of place. He felt small, a lot smaller than his 156 centimeters at the time, a few months short of being age fourteen. An overdressed stuffy fellow wearing white gloves and a black suit with dovetails reminded Sepp that he was outside his territory. “You have no business to be in the front of the house, go do your assigned work.” He said in a low, almost whispering voice.

Halfheartedly, Sepp trudged in the direction of the kitchen, to his silver-cleaning area. Sepp faced the two doors separating the heavenly guest-side and the doomed back of the house. After carefully choosing the door that did not get much use, the one to his left, Sepp kicked the copper-clad door with his strong soccer legs wide open. He did it the same way he had seen the waiters do it. Everybody heard the impact. Above Sepp was a tray, airborne. Behind it, a waiter was slamming into the door. What happened? Should Sepp maybe have tried the other door to get back into the kitchen? The crash-boom, a-clack, a-clunk had overshadowed the loud slam-bang of the waiter's body against the door's edge. The tray's contents followed the laws of gravity. A metal plate cover came with a clink-clunk to rest at Sepp's right foot. Meat, vegetables, garnishes, and sauces, next to a not yet filleted whole fish, looked most unappetizing between the covers and sharp pointed pieces of once expensive china. Dark brown and sticky yellow sauces were dripping from the off-white painted door and its frame.

In the midst of the most unappetizing food display on the floor, keeping the door ajar was a momentarily helpless human being. It was the same waiter who had earlier offered to bring Sepp the Sidol. He was sitting amidst the mess and looked out of place in his black patent leather shoes, black socks, black tuxedo pants, the starched white shirt, a black bowtie, and his black dovetail jacket. What about the bunch of parsley in his hair? "Ja! How did it get there, how odd" Sepp's confusion lasted only a second. Sepp was going to say: "Ja! I went looking for you. I'm sorry. I didn't mean to do you harm.

You must know it was the door's fault." However, Sepp didn't get to say more than "Ja!" An endless cacophony of shouted words came from the kitchen. It was the Chef de Cuisine, who was jumping up and down, waving a two-pronged dangerous looking utensil in his hand. "Oh ... grande merde!" "What did you do with my food?" The Chef cook was threatening the speechless waiter. He promised to take every cent out of the server's tips. He also said he wouldn't rest until the damage was all paid for in full. The poor fellow in the penguin outfit slowly raised himself off the floor and brushed the garnish from his hair. Apparently, in great pain, he limped off, holding onto his rear end.

A dishwasher and two maids cleaned up after the accident. Within minutes it was all back to normal. The incident barely interrupted the steady stream of waiters going into the kitchen and coming out as business started to pick up again. Young, inexperienced, trying to do the right thing and to ease his guilt feelings, as a God-fearing Catholic, Sepp went to the chef. Although waited till after the same had put the large meat fork down, and Sepp confessed his mistake. The Chef de Cuisine listened, then looked at Sepp and started to call him names, many of these names the boy had never heard before. It must have been some French dialect. Now Sepp was rightfully scared. Sepp didn't dare to go any place, but back to his corner. Here in the silver cleaning area, Sepp found two fresh bottles of Sidol, and all he did that first day was cleaning and polishing silver. Sepp didn't mind the petroleum smell, and that his hands were all black and dirty. It was long past lunch hour that an older waiter asked him: "You had lunch already?" and seeing Sepp's face, he knew the answer. "You hungry?" And not waiting to hear Sepp's "Ja! I had a piece of bread earlier that was for breakfast. Yes, I am hungry!" that friendly waiter brought him some most delicious leftovers he scraped from two silver platters onto a regular dinner plate. There was a piece of meat and vegetables, and three roasted, parsley covered small potatoes. Just seeing it, Sepp instantly felt better. And he ate it all while listening to some waiter's tales told to him by the waiter, who had been waiting tables for more than 50 years.

Aside the run-in with the door, all day 10 hours Sepp cleaned silver. That was a long day.

By nightfall, Otto found Sepp still polishing silver. Before leaving work, Otto showed him where to get soap, to take back to their living space. They did so by raiding two of the guest bathrooms. Otto also took a roll of toilette paper and asked Sepp to stuff one in his shirt too, saying: “I was told that we have to buy our very own toilette paper when I asked for some supplies. Sepp, at 20DM a month, I don’t have money to spare on the bathroom!” Then they went back to their room, and yes Sepp needed a lot of soap to clean his hands.

Sepp was tired, and he slept deep and good.

The second day on the job, Sepp took a break from silver cleaning. He was looking for Otto. Somehow he got into one of the banquet rooms. A banquet was in full swing. Fifty or so people in long dresses, suits, and ties, were having dinner. Fascinated, Sepp watched. At the table closest to him, a waiter balanced a huge silver platter on his left hand and forearm. Using a large fork and a big spoon, he transferred meat slices onto each guest's plate. A second waiter followed him with a vegetable platter even bigger than the one holding the meat. He too served just the right amount onto each customer's plate.

Sepp counted and recounted. There were five tables of ten, and two waiters served the food each table. All went like clockwork. The waiters didn’t talk to each other. Nobody was giving them commands. Each of them knew what to do. Sepp imagined himself out there soon, waiting on tables just like them, and being close to these rich folks and dignitaries. Sepp knew waiting on tables paid well, and he was excited about the idea to get to see a class of people which he would otherwise never have met while living in Kleinerort. Yesterday, late afternoon, an older waiter had told Sepp a few stories about his work experiences. He was speaking about the dignitaries such as the Herrenvolk, Royal families, heads of states and stage stars he had waited on over the years. Sepp was impressed. Because he had heard Sepp’s stomach growling, he had brought him some leftover food from a party.

While watching the party in full swing, to be less noticeable, Sepp stepped back. His stomach started to make noises again. The massive four to eight-foot-thick walls within the more than thousand-year-old sandstone building presented spacious doorways. They were at least four times the size of their outhouse back home.

That doorway was sparsely lit. Sepp felt safe and entirely hidden from the guests' eyes. He had found a perfect spot for his observations. Here he was out of sight of the steady flow of waiters, who entered and left the room on the far end, the kitchen side. Nosy, standing on his toes, Sepp spied through the round windows in the door behind him. He recognized, on the other side, the empty bar and lounge area.

Sepp stood with his back to the door, completely occupied mentally, fascinated, he took in the whole panorama of the dining event. The five tables were arranged in an open oval under the many multifaceted glittering cut glass pieces of two massive chandeliers. The guests sat on red-upholstered, white-painted wooden Windsor style chairs. The white linen on the table in front of them was loaded with different glasses, silver candle holders, and flower arrangements. Surefooted waiters floated between the tables.

Chitter-chatter, gibble-gabble, and here and there a yak and some yakkity-yak filled the air. The clink-clanks of glasses meeting each other, here and there knives and forks clicking on the plates, and seeing the food made him hungry. He hadn't had much to eat since his arrival at the most beautiful of the local hotels. A rich-looking woman was slurping full-size spears of asparagus. Holding the green vegetable just the right way with her asparagus tongs, she nibbled, and then she sucked half a spear into her mouth, a gentle bite, slurp-slurp. Drips of butter were taking a trip dribbling from one chin to the next one before being transformed into a perfect gloss, rubbed by her forearm onto her skin. Nothing slowed her down. Her eating utensil grabbed another long thin green asparagus. Head first she sucked it down. There was no meat on her plate. 'Herbivores,' so Sepp thought while looking at her table partner, the one with the Schnitzel, 'Carnivorous.' Sepp's mouth, a few minutes earlier dry and thirsting, was now filling with saliva, and his belly made most unmistakable growling sounds. Starving, he watched with mixed feelings. Sepp needed some food. A growling stomach noise confirmed his cravings. Nevertheless, much excited about his discovery, Sepp thought: “Here in the room with the customers, that’s where I want to be—floating over the carpets like these waiters, I too want to be on the floor, and not hidden away in the dungeon, cleaning silver and...”

Crack, bang crash! The door hit Sepp hard in the back. He tumbled forward and fell on his knees, right in front of the first table. Bad timing for a prayer! “Oh Scheisse!” he uttered in pain. Glass was exploding all around him, shattering into many pieces. It had a high musical pitch to it. Sepp didn’t know that it was the sound of crystal breaking. Then the noise yielded to a calm, a near complete silence, except for a few muffled sounds from the last table. Young Sepp had the guests' undivided attention. Everyone looked in his direction. They all heard the wine waiter's shouting voice: "*Dummkopf, ...Saubloeder Hammel,” and “dummer Hund...”* he was cussing vigorously.

Panic-stricken, Sepp wished to become invisible, be able to go into hiding, maybe in a flowerpot. Huge clay pots with exotic plants were close by, and desperately he was looking for a ‘vacancy’ sign. But Sepp had to face reality. He felt the people's eyes pointing at him, the surprise doorstopper. However, they were able to figure out that the waiter carrying a full tray of glasses, coming from the bar, had not seen him standing in front of the door. The waiter was still using profanities, a second waiter, or was it the bartender had joined. Both were on their knees sweeping glass-fragments from the floor onto a tray. Sepp offered to help, picking up glass with his hands only to be told *“Hanswurst get out of here!”* and *“Crawl back in the hole you came from and never come back to my station.”*The two waiter persons had strong accents, their cursing one in Bayrish and one in Schwäbish was just too funny sounding. Even Sepp who was getting up from the floor couldn’t hide a grin from his face. A woman giggled, then another joined in, and the hearty laughter contagiously caught on. They were not angry with Sepp. He knew they laughed about the wine waiter's and the bartender’s most hilarious use of language. They had sympathy for the young fellow’s stupidity. Sepp looked around. Now he saw the red painted area on the floor where he had been standing earlier, which was supposed to signal: “Stay clear of any red area in front of the door.” Sepp had found out the hard way what it meant. He retreated to his silver cleaning section without saying a word. His superiors forgave him once more.

On day 3, Sepp didn’t dare to move from the silver-cleaning station in the back of the hotel’s preparation kitchen, except to make the trip to the employees’ bathroom. Earlier the Chef de Cuisine called him ‘Diablo’ while pointing at him. Sepp washed his hands carefully. He used a lot of water, as there was no cleanser to clean his hands. The ‘rotten-egg-silver-cleaner-smell’ was hard to get off his skin without some soap. The towel hanging on the wall was soaking wet already. He figured it out that rubbing his hands on the towel got much of the Sidol of his fingers, but all it did was leaving dark marks on the cloth.

Before he went to the bathroom, Sepp had asked one of the waiters, "Ja! What does ‘Diablo’ mean?" "Devil," was the answer. Returning to his corner in the very back of the kitchen, Sepp tried to slip by unnoticed. At the kitchen pick-up line, the Maitre d'hotel and the Chef cornered him. Sepp's back was toward the kitchen counter. It was hot and humid in the kitchen. The air was laden with a variety of pleasant smells from roasts in the ovens and the always-simmering stockpots on the stoves. Sepp was hungry. His stomach was growling again. Sepp had loved all the cooking smells at first. However, right now he despised them. The heat was rising. Sweat pearls started their steady drip under his arms. He felt the water running down his back, caught in the furrow between his buttocks, he was uncomfortable, to say the least.

Sepp was afraid, shivering on the inside and sweating on the outside. Unable to go anyplace, he listened: "...Sepp, we doubt that you have what it takes to become a waiter." The Chef de Cuisine had a lot more to say, but nothing good at all. The Chef was taking inventory of Sepp's lack of good qualities, and it was a long list. Behind the Chef's back, Sepp noticed the cooks laughing. They enjoyed the show as Sepp was publicly reprimanded. In Sepp's mind to be tarred and feathered couldn't have been worse than what he was going through right now then and there. His butthole puckered.

To Sepp's surprise, the Maitre d' spoke out in his favor. “Gentlemen! It’s our fault, a lack of proper training. Let’s now work together.” Turning to Sepp he said: "One more complaint from anyone here, and I shall wring your neck before I throw you out! You hear me, Sepp?” “Good-for-nothing. He doesn’t deserve another chance...! Look at him, ...useless trash.” was the Chef’s comment.

Lucky for him, a busy waiter came to Sepp’s rescue. He carried above his left shoulder a full tray loaded with dinners and another tray on his right hand. “Eh! Son! Eh! You! Can you follow me with the Gulyas soup?” Speechless, Sepp nodded. Finally, somebody recognized his unlimited potential. They needed and wanted his help. Now the Maitre d' pointed at the large soup tureen. And he gave Sepp specific instructions: “Pick it up with both hands and just follow him. Listen! Use only the doors to your right. And never stand in any red-marked area. You understand? Go!” The devil hiding his horns under the tall white chef’s hat, camouflaged in a white cook's jacket, added: "If you drop that. I kill you myself."

Sure of his abilities and able to follow instructions Sepp was going to show them. His strength and good spirits returned as quickly as they had vanished. Proud and sure of himself, with vigor and no second thoughts, hastily he grabbed both handles of the large silver soup bowl. Sepp lifted it from the kitchen counter, chest-high, only to watch it fly. It hit the manager above the knee. The Gulyas soup was now running over the Maitre de's shoes. At the moment, the silver soup tureen hit the floor, long before its lid came to a rest, Sepp's painful screams were echoing between the white tiled kitchen walls: "Autsch! That's hot! Oh, Scheisse!" But his burnt fingers were not the most important, as he dashed past the momentarily stunned superiors. Sepp sprinted out the kitchen's delivery entrance, slaloming between purveyors. His mind was telling him to run for his life. Sepp expected flying knives from the chef. He knew if his superiors got hold of him they most likely would make him suffer horribly for his wrongdoings. Afraid of torture, and he was acutely aware that those old towns had medieval torture chambers. Maybe they had an "Eiserne Jungfrau" (Iron Maiden torture device) as he had seen at a castle his school had visited. However, Sepp had enough sense to stop in, down the road where he rushed up to his kammer and got his little suitcase with the second shirt and the spare shoes and socks. Sepp also grabbed his beloved lederhosen and stuffed them into the rucksack, then left in a great hurry. He was walking fast, and here and there ran, and only slowed down after he had passed the north gate of the walled city.

Breathing hard, outside the town’s walls Sepp had to stop, still in his work uniform. Sepp no longer noticed that he was hungry. While trying to catch his breath, he opened his rucksack and checked the pockets of his lederhosen. He counted the coins, and all were there. Sepp felt a great relief when he spotted the blue and white bus. Sepp was glad he hadn't had time to spend any of his money yet because it was just enough to pay for the bus ticket back home to Kleinerort.

Blowing air onto the big blisters on both his hands and fingers he was. Yes, those blisters were the only souvenirs he brought back home from the medieval town. It took some time for the lesson to sink in. While on the bus home, Sepp in his mind knew "Ja! Accidents do happen, they always happen." Sepp didn't run away from his duties as an apprentice. He ran to save his life because the evil forces had ganged up against him. The Chef de Cuisine, the Maitre d', the cooks, the waiters, the hotel owner, the doorman and everybody else were trying to get him. There were too many of them. And they were stronger too, therefore defeated, Sepp knew he had to retreat, only to regroup and try again. Sepp's mind was set. He was going to become a waiter. He was going to travel the world. He was going to become rich and famous, in spite of what those dressed-up stuffed shirts back there at the Luxury Hotel had said and thought of him.

Seven weeks later, the blisters were gone, his hands had healed. Sepp started his next apprenticeship as a waiter, far away from Altestadt, and far away from Kleinerort, up north in the Hansestadt. Sepp was not going to make the same mistakes again. After several weeks of thinking about and reliving his actions in Altestadt, he had learned a lot from his initially awkward behaviors while at the Luxury Hotel in Altestadt.

On the day before Sepp left for the Hansestadt, Waldemar, his father received a letter from the Red Cross about some members of his family he had left behind in Sudetenland, and they were now living in East Germany. "Manfred and my sister both are alive! Oh, God! They are in East Germany!" Waldemar said and retreated into his shoemaker shop, and locked the door behind him. When Sepp knocked he got the answer of: "Go away Sepp, I need some time alone!"

...signs of the times...

With this Oh yes does he recall being
and her attracting males so easily
during these sixties and seventies. Let
her believe she is the best. He does live
with her. She calls the pill "diet", men "staple". Learn
sex is good. "The more, the better is life"
she says appropriately. "Hon make love."
Sparsely lit places, those niches of lust

have him worry that it's going to hell
if she keeps on visiting all those hav'ns
but he goes along wherev'r go she shall.

helmut s